Notes from Plato's Cave

Reina Attias

TRAFFORD
PUBLISHING™

Note for Librarians: A cataloguing record for this book is available from Library and Archives Canada at www.collectionscanada.ca/amicus/index-e.html

ISBN: 978-1-4251-0494-8 (sc)

Printed in Victoria, BC, Canada. Printed on paper with minimum 30% recycled fibre. Trafford's print shop runs on "green energy" from solar, wind and other environmentally-friendly power sources.

Trafford rev. 7/2/2009

   www.trafford.com

Book sales for North America and international:
Trafford Publishing, 6E–2333 Government St.,
Victoria, BC V8T 4P4 CANADA
phone 250 383 6864 (toll-free 1 888 232 4444)
fax 250 383 6804; email to orders@trafford.com

Order online at:
www.trafford.com

... The tale has been saved and has not perished and will save us if we are obedient to the word and we shall pass safely over the river of forgetfulness and our soul will not be defiled.

The Republic
Plato

ONE

IT STARTS OUT LIKE a stone – perfectly round, possessing no striations containing no fissures – no entry point. She knows the Analyst is not truly a stone; she also knows that this recurring image blocks the narrative.

The story, the struggle to narrate fastens onto a phrase about women coined by the early Church Father Tertullian that went something like this – woman – earthly, actual woman, that is, awakened to her nature, is janua diaboli 'the devil's door.' This is comforting – an explanation of the ambivalence in creating the narrative; in producing the descriptive text and casting it into the silence; into the world of the dead voices whispering in the weekly confrontations.

She trudges to the Analyst. She refuses to lie down on the couch. She sits in a chair, covers herself with a blanket –freezing – and wonders, where is my blood? She tries to be bright/clever to appease this Stone the Analyst – to be like Moses striking a rock – but the water does not come. She selects/edits/resists the flood of words, a true utterance would be catastrophic, her blood drains away, her feet are blocks of ice, her teeth chatter. Finally the session is over.

That's that. However, the book starts out elsewhere. In the aftermath of madness, in a voice on a tightrope not touching the ground, words flying through the air for the audience. Words to fool the watchers, a sleight of hand. A voice rising hysterically in an approved sanity.

When she emerged from the hospital, stunned and drugged, flayed, the air a rough intrusion, an assault, the voice spoke in the long afternoons like clockwork, like an appointment. It said; it described; it represented a dialectic; it pretended a subject. It spoke in a foreign language; it uttered words, sentences, throwing them up like rotten meat, frantic to be all there could ever be of writing. Still, it is the way into the book – backwards into the madness seen from no–where, seen from hysteria fleeing from itself, seen from above the abyss of a body without parts. It speaks only in words; it begins at recapitulation, in the stratosphere of an American Dream of a perfect adjustment to being crazy. So it won't disturb the ground, won't dig up, dig in, fall into a crevice, flail into the waiting darkness.

And now, barely arriving at these assignations with Analyst, the voice no longer speaks itself on the page; it has become merely a symptom. Still, it must be exhumed, presented, copied out again, here, because that is the beginning. At the center, the mid–point of going mad.

It opens the narrative like this; the guilty narrative, sly and secret from that Stone who Knows. knows but does not know, must not know these words.

❋

This is the first time I've been able to sit down and write since I came out of the hospital. Dr. Feingold insisted that the stress and strain of my personal relationships had finally pushed me over the edge. "After all," he said smiling his best smile and trying not to appear too patronizing, "you're not a psychiatrist."

Some of my friends thought that it was the pernicious influence of the women's group, which six of us had kept going for over six years. "What can you expect," they said, "talking about all that stuff in that ingrown atmosphere."

On the other hand, the idea persisted that what had actually precipitated my "breakdown" was the sudden exposure to nature in the form of a weekend visit to a lovely mountain retreat in the company of some good old friends. Of course, nobody wanted to actually call it a breakdown and so the euphemisms abounded – break–through, psychic implosion, psychic explosion, psychotic episode. What everyone seemed to be able to agree upon, including the hospital staff and members of the psychological profession, was that *something* had definitely happened. I would agree with that.

One of the most valuable pieces of fallout was the book I had been working on before this something happened. The idea persisted that hidden in the words I had so laboriously put down on paper lay the real clue to my psychic workings, which were now lying in a scrambled heap at my feet. In addition, I was certainly attached to the characters, painstakingly etched on bits of paper and stuffed into various notebooks. But when I retrieved these bits, a rather obvious metaphor for the bits of myself scattered in the debris of the happening, these very characters were strangers.

Actually, why does Marguerita, one of the most important elements have to die? Die and suffer a peculiar resurrection in a frightened Angelica? So then, why did I, scribbling on pieces of envelopes, secret even from myself, murder Marguerita?

I was utterly convinced, up to and including the moment when three armed guards, several friends and my husband – after trying to convince me to take some medicine to no avail – carried me kicking, hollering and biting off to the hospital, that given time I could work out the puzzle, grasp the network of all the relationships I had ever had in my life. I was sure that through a process of logic and analysis, I could at last be certain that these were the good guys, those the bad; could determine what kind of programming I had received, undo it and emerge whole, like Athena out of the head of Zeus. What happened instead, was that my perceptual faculties unraveled to their first beginnings and I did not know whether it was day or night or whether I was gazing at the sun or moon.

So much for logical deduction.

The shadows continue to gyrate and the light reveals more darkness; perhaps my dispensing with Marguerita pales in significance. Here in Plato's Cave, shadow is substance and substance a chimera.

Dot.. Dot. Dot. Marguerita, Daisy, Maggie, in all her name transformations and Angelica, Angel, Mary, as I say somewhere in the writings, are two halves of the same whole and clearly that whole is the narrator I discovered to carry the book, and more than likely the narrator is me. So there are four of us, Angelica, Maggie, the Narrator and me.

The Men:

During my five day stay at the hospital and after I was released, I was afraid of everything, but particularly men. I felt that I had forfeited myself and now was really in the hands of the enemy, a prisoner of war. The hospital staff smiled, but I knew what they were thinking. Some of the female nurses were on their side while some of the male nurses were not. So while gender was paramount, even gender could fool you.

There was another division, a magical reference point by which I calculated if someone was friend or enemy and even that could change

PARANOIA

From what dark corner of my slowly dissolving ego had these malevolent figures arrived? Had they always been there, unconsciously causing a side– step dance in my behavior? Or did they arrive like vultures, at the first signs of the decay of my defense systems?

So the book started out with five people on an island in Greece. Two women and three men. Gradually it reduced itself to a quadrille, as the fifth figure could never reach consciousness. Still, five seems a better number than four. On the other hand, Dr. Jung says that four is the number of wholeness. The configurations of the mandala that the psyche keeps producing ad infinitum all over the world symbolic of wholeness, the Self.

Some sages and even shrinks disagree and believe that three is the correct number for wholeness. Four is feminine and three is masculine according to some systems. Also there is an ongoing dispute over the meaning of seven, eight, and nine. And some people have arguments going about the ten system and the twelve system. Everybody thinks thirteen is a generally unlucky number to be avoided. Especially if we see it as the number of the devil – which obviously would be a combination of the impure 10 and the defeminized 3. Apparently the number 1,153 is fairly neutral; however the numbers 1,080 and 108 actually have mystical significance.

The quadrille. A dance from medieval Europe or maybe Lewis Carroll, in which four people move in and out among each other in a mystifying fashion, changing partners and smiling all the while. There is occasional hand–clapping and foot stomping. And so the book resolved to four: Maggie, Angelica, Alex, and Jean–Claude.

The men:

Alex is an architect. And Alex is one of the beautiful people. Now that could get complicated. He's not like a wolf in sheep's clothing at all. He might be a mythical monster in wolf's clothing. Or perhaps a fox is better, in spite of the fact that the fox spirit in both China and Japan is always feminine. You see the teeth; the flick of the tail out of the corner of your eye – but you can't believe it. Can't believe that something so beautiful, bright and shiny, clean and wholesome could really have a bushy red tail emerging out of the seat of his perfectly fitted chino pants.

But that's only the smallest hint of what Alex is about. As long as you are near him you always feel like you are just about to reach the top of Everest and plant a flag. Alex plays push-pull. *He beckons you run. You reach him he turns away. You touch him he moves two steps north. You stop. He beckons, repeat from *. You turn away. * He comes up behind you and lifts you off your feet. You turn around. He moves two steps west. You stop confused. He beckons. Repeat from *.

Alex is a trap.

He steals bodies, words, imagination, volition.
Then he doles out our own attributes to us in sanitized parcels.
Maggie can eat five of him for breakfast. Can't she?

When they had me in the first set of restraints at the hospital, I was convinced that the whole event was designed to create the first female messiah. Christ had come to teach men. I was here to lead the way for women. I was going to get crucified so that other women would never have to go through it again. The entire hospital staff and doctors from major think tanks and the Menninger Clinic, in league with Giant Computers in the East, all were monitoring my every movement – physical and mental – through an elaborate series of electrodes.

Each gesture re–programmed a section of my cortex and the final result of this re– programming was to be the "new woman", the model for other women without them having to go through the suffering I was experiencing. The free woman with all the parts fully functioning – with all the aspects society had repressed liberated and operative.

Obviously with that kind of Weltanschauung it was imperative that I free myself of all the restraints. First the right wrist, then the left wrist, followed by the right ankle. Just as I was about to undo the left ankle, a friend came into the emergency room. I looked up at her and shouted whoopee! Whoopee because at last we were all free. The cortex had been reprogrammed, the crucifixion had been accomplished, and the resurrection was at hand I did not have to die as I had feared and be ritualistically consumed.

The end result of my integrative experience was that I was put in triple restraints and the drugs began to finally take effect.

Maggie keeps spinning in ever smaller circles creating a magnificent design on the smallest conceivable space between an endless corridors of double binds. Because I fear that she moves on the tiniest whirl of the pointing forefinger of Michelangelo's God the Father, she is in grave danger of being destroyed by Alex.

※

Another voice, the subject, interjects itself, attempts acrobatics to deflect the text, to subvert the narrative inevitably unfolding under the madness, under the flight from the story. Nevertheless it does remember; took pictures, made snapshots, recorded, was a camera with a voice over, over now forever? The island is moving toward the mainland after a volcanic eruption – she can say that much to the Analyst/detective –and also recount dreams never contexted which now become entrances.

The Analyst diligently records the dreams. There is some kind of public building. A lot of people all actively doing different things, bustling with papers, eating together, talking. Suddenly the dreamer becomes aware that she alone is transparent, this seems to cause panic although no–one else pays attention. The dreamer rushes over to a large desk with the words INFORMATION on a black and white plaque. In almost a whisper she asks the man behind the desk, where is my life? He looks right past (through) her smiling. She asks again, louder and again louder until she wakes up wet with anxiety, hair pasted to the back of her neck. After that there is no–one to speak to and no words to speak.

One morning in the distant past in the midst of a black depression, a vision appeared: the image of a ratty old woman in front of a fire. There was darkness all around her and people listening to her words for she was wise.

---

old woman they said
tell us a story of love   of death
of high adventure   She sighed and arranged her
dirty skirts around bulky knees
eyes penetrating the lowering fire her voice wa
s   surprisingly soft and moved
gently as a flute   of love I can tell the
many kinds   mother for child of fathers and
sons   of adolescents   of husbands and wives
of lovers and more   and of death too coming
suddenly to the body   slowly to the soul
of black death that leaves ashes
of red death that is like a phoenix and others you
don't want to know   of high adventure only one
the soul questing   as for the rest you must ask
old men about battles and angry horses and swords
they story what was or is or might be   I tell of
changes of   shadows   of light   I tell of the shape
changer in the   soul

TWO

IN A SMALL ROOM STRAINING to listen, fearing an attack, the assault of an alien utterance, she grasps at the facility of madness, the already written words of a book. Is it spoken here? Or is it delivered in an envelope later? Hammered out, pounded in against the resistance to re–see it, to see it otherwise. It is finally not saying anything. It is saying it all in a mirror.

Someone insists that this is not the beginning, in spite of the hope that it does in fact open here. She sees Analyst as a nemesis. She sees a spiraling back to the slowly disintegrating seed of this flower. The madness presented as a theater of madness. Then the tension is complete. The opposites invisible, generating mute stasis. Staring at space filling the room drifting in absence

It is always a shock to see the Analyst. Each time the adrenaline spurts as the door opens. She then vanishes in the blackness of the ceiling and words form – no narrative is possible, all continuity is erased. The words recount a dream, an event; she pulls the afghan up to her chin, a gesture only, there is no body there. She barely thinks – do you love me? –She barely feels something forming that if she had a narrative, if there were memory, she would call terror. Still, there is a kind of movement; a balance. A raid on the arsenal of words. Stolen from old Notes, the characters sluggishly break through and Angelica writes:

"What is it about the wreck of a man, like a derelict ship, that so attracts women? Is it the hope of buried treasure? Or something less material; the dream of being useful, of saving the abandoned ruin?"

So a narrative, a story with its back broken has been there all along. This is never spoken to the Analyst. There is no subject. Yet according to the great French psychiatrist, it goes something like this: ...the language speaks the subject, the speaker is subjected to language rather than the master of it.

So it all will have been, will be spoken by words, by breath, by spirit. Now only cacophony, a babble of voices, the book and the madness mixed still to be at some future moment distilled. Nevertheless it continues, all the noises, the sounds of battle. She is a historian.

❋

Hillman says the problem is that we have a monolithic concept of ego. A heroic concept. A Freudian concept. Where ID was EGO shall be. Nevertheless everyone keeps telling me my ego is fragile right now. I prefer mutable. Once upon a time at a dinner party, a young intense man was giving us a rundown on the happenings at a humanistic psychology holistic psychic consciousness expanding conference in California.

"And finally we decided that the eagle must be destroyed. The eagle is the enemy."

"The eagle? But why?"

Everyone stared at me. "Not EAGLE you asshole, EGO, EGO."

It is said after all that the characters in a book are aspects of the author's ego. It is said that the book is the working out of psychic contents that in fact go beyond ego to encompass the realm of archetypes of the collective unconscious. For example, Heathcliff in Wuthering Heights is the ghostly lover animus of Emily Bronte and in this manner the animas and animuses of writers wander through novels impersonating characters. From the standpoint of a mutable ego however, a non–heroic ego, who is Emily Bronte?

Possibly I murdered Maggie because it provided a curious way to do a post mortem on complex relationships by removing the possibility of change. The film strip is suddenly cut and that's it....no more takes. Earlier on I mentioned my fear that Maggie could be destroyed by Alex. I repudiate that. Alex could be seen as a convenient male type for both Maggie and Angelica to try out their budding consciousness on. To play off against, to overcome, to defeat, to surpass. In that case Maggie's death and resurrection in Angelica represents a hopeful situation. A situation that echoes the experience in the emergency room of the hospital. An experience in which the continuous fragmentation of our selves is finally healed. Double think is banished forever along with considerations of what will please anyone, offend anyone. We then view ourselves as a natural phenomenon, a hurricane or earthquake, drought or flood. Is this possible? And if it were, is it desirable?

Indeed. I came out of the hospital on a Thursday. I considered that it was my extraordinary intelligence and sly ways that got me released – particularly reading Thursday the Rabbi Walked Out, a detective story which was clearly the game plan of my escape. My husband purchased that book reasonably certain that it was sufficiently neutral to avoid triggering a relapse.

I was a wreck. However, unlike some men, as Angelica writes, I was not a derelict ship yet; but approaching or leaving the dangerous Saragossa Sea. My ego wasn't mutable at that time – it had gone on an extended holiday. I had no idea who the house sitters were –they came and went without notice. That reminds me of Marguerita – but she's dead before this book begins –nevertheless there is no book without her voice. Marguerita on relationships says:

"You think you make love like an animal because you are too passionate, too lost in the act. You are wrong. You cannot make love like an animal at all. What you do is the all too human act of forgetting. You forget in the moment you reach climax, you forget when you are having your dinner. I don't mean merely remembering your passion and becoming excited again. I mean this gap... we always relate horizontally – between one event and the other which makes it easier to forget. Have you ever watched animals? They copulate without passion – just as they eat without greed. Leave the animals to themselves. We stumble because we forget."

"You get out of bed and put your pants on. You forget. The scenery shifts and you are looking at another film in which this event is not included. You look at me and wonder who I am, how I got here. You don't remember that we are, were, we will be in bed, at dinner, apart, dead. You think we are walking on a road and the scenery moves past us, but we are floating in the sea and the sea is flowing in our veins...."

It is true that in the week preceding my admittance to the hospital, every significant relationship I had ever had in my life, from the most mundane to the celestial realms, lost anchor and floated away in the dark of night: a Quixotic armada composed of row boats, sailing ships, motor ships, rafts, rubber tubes and massive ocean liners. That metaphor fails unless we imagine that while all that was happening – The Great God of the Sea led by Proteus created the mixed media show of all time.

Nothing is brought to the Stone – no Notes, no book, no story – only the learned words, the invention of history – no origins appear in this language. This she calls "autobiography". But even this is a step into the unknown. She is left a construction worker; an unwilling archeologist secretly afraid of a curse. Nevertheless she must listen to this voice..

In the book I made a mistake. The others were just shadows – the Greeks, the Swiss. Undeveloped elements in the fixated drama taking place between the four on the island. And one of the many titles was Landfall – the first sighting of land. I shunned political reference points. Perhaps these characters, rather than being parts of me, were in fact not parts of me – they lived on Jules Verne's mysterious island.

And Dr. Feingold triggered the remembrance of the island when he said that I had obviously been "pushed over the edge". I wondered even then, the edge of what? What can you expect from a Neo– Freudian. I was under the impression that the world was round. Maybe the world isn't round. There are other views. Who knows what the Fiji Islanders think or anyone for that matter. Clearly Dr. Feingold doesn't realize he doubts the world is round. But where are the stars and what separates the heavens from the earth? I had been given warnings from the island, omens.

She sneaks a peek, in the dead of night, at a letter Maggie wrote. as if she were a panicky thief, fleeing from pursuers.

"Angel:

Beach, wind, mousy sea, mousy sky, no cat, no tension, saw my footprints, a straight line disappearing – sand hard packed cement streaked with grease. Five people in a restaurant stared at me – crazy American.. a motor bike rumbling in the distance then across the sand avoiding waves. Odd assortment of debris – everything broken. Drew a history of voyages with an old branch, old faces.

Why this prelude you ask to damnation?

Because it's connected to that sea tunnel of a day, the black sand, myself an empty cup bobbing out, out, no waves. Stopped at a restaurant barbuine, horte, tomatoes, feta even the sun came out. I was still bobbing should I have been surprised then at the apparitions?

They walked up to the restaurant slowly, as if they weren't really coming, the younger behind the elder, medieval text on crusades, no–color skirts, weskits blue and red with gold trimming, ragged dirty blouses, black scarves with fringes over their heads, faces brown, sullen, very crafty. They stopped suddenly as if there were a fence in front of them and quietly stood there with their hands out. I knew they were coming for me."

Angelica knew then that it was a message from the mysterious island, for she says: I am she and I am dying. I feel the curse of dark things following me, demanding, seeking, like those gypsies.

❊

She considers the radical differences; the voice of the Notes, the voices in the book, the non–voice in the Analyst's office. The separations and fences – defenses. The topography without Time or Space. She considers without issue – thinking of curses, of omens, of dangers in utterance of any kind. She reads for comfort. "Having established the principle that the text could be approached like a dream, that we could interpret one element at a time rather than feel responsible for understanding the totality..." Then she can manage to continue – in an impermeable silence, only allowing the interjections of madness.

In fairy tale terms, I was bewitched. Under the spell of a dark magician or perhaps an evil witch. Maggie and Angelica had been banished to a desert island; the end of the world; the desolate place. But the messages continued to come. In bottles, in dreams, in accidents and ailments, in depressions and anxiety and finally in breakdown – when at last, like the fabled Atlantis the submerged continent of which the island is but a part surfaced. She holds the paper in her hand, the paper holding the words that Angelica wrote and without reason, she finds herself crying.

"She was my sister in the truest sense of that word – the mythic sense. Gilgamesh and Enkidu and all the brothers in fairy tales, the one full of light, the other clumsy, beastly, often stupid, saving each other, killing each other, fooling each other, exchanging shadows, egos, death and life, moving in a mobius strip of mirrors in which their multiple faces confront them in astonished recognition."

THREE

THE COUCH HAS BECOME more familiar to her –
an experience of awful vulnerability –even with the
autobiography as a cover. The confusion is in the
body; races through the flesh.

The Analyst is there, an invisible presence/absence
watching her. Looking at her on the couch fabricating
a body, elaborating, translating an experience of
madness, of a book, of writings that have existed before.
This seems better than nothing. The authoritative eye
will discern the shape of the discourse. Only her eyes
flutter, blink rapidly avoiding the penetrating gaze.
The patient is powerless to see, the patient is filled
with blindness.

The body of the patient is a sickness, is confused,
is a place of heresy, flat on her back on the couch,
on a bed. She begins to suspect that all writings are
part of the analysis. There's the description of events
within the boundaries of the office; then there is the
wilderness – a place beyond, but inscribed here as
well. Traced in the flight of words, visible in the gaps,
apparent as mad verbosity.

From that wilderness Angelica writes to Alex:

"The endless description of events, the kind of historical accumulation of more and more facts about ourselves never leads us toward an understanding – toward understanding the story. This attempt to apprehend reality through addition has the reverse effect. It leads us round and round collecting endlessly. It's mathematics. We need subtraction through spirals to zero. A zero which bursts through time into eternity."

That it seems is what the Analyst wants from her – but the Analyst occasionally socializes with Dr.Feingold; the Analyst sits out of sight; the office can never be the wilderness. The fences are too strong. And she is secretly glad. She trembles on the verge but the mad images intervene, contravene the tenuous constructed reality of the analysis. Having read something on Narration in the Psychoanalytic Dialogue, she determines that in fact Analyst is also telling a story. Although the story is being told in a rule governed manner, she finds certain words elicit responses, certain tellings create a momentary dialogue.

However this is not speech. The flesh body refuses all language, perversely clings to the incantations intoned when the body fell into itself, into the hands of the enemy.

During the inquisition Giordano Bruno defied the Inquisition racing across Europe and even as far as England – until finally he challenged them in Italy, where they caught him and according to the custom of the times burned him at the stake. That was 1600 A.D. The hospital authorities, the shrinks, the nurses had the power, while I, drugged and the patient clearly had none. Mere administers of medication or leaders of group therapy or bringers of bedpans wield this magic.

It was a matter of life and death not to let 'them' find out that I too 'knew'. Knew what power really controlled the hospital and everyone in it. At all cost I had to be sure that I appeared to be on the side of that power and innocent of its existence at the same time. There is secular power and non–secular power. In theocratic states the distinction is non–existent. The Divine King is the sole representative of God on earth, both the repository and representative of all power. Similarly, Christ compares the Heavenly Father with the earthly father "Which of you if his child asks for bread will give him a stone?" Which of you? Which of you give her stones? Which of you embed rocks in her flesh? Alex is a purveyor of stones. Maggie keeps throwing them back in his face. Angelica tries to eat them all.

This illuminates an aspect of her essential muteness; following which the Stone forms breasts. At the very beginning there was a respite; as in a bedtime story heard only once, then the voice of the Mother fades like a melody drowned forever in the sea. That was how the mad voice sang the images into being at the beginning, a priori. And when she came out of the hospital, the insistent voice recorded it.

The psychic explosion began with an ecstatic vision of Demeter/Persephone figured in a votary candle with the Virgin of Guadalupe luridly painted on its side. She was the Mother of Everything Living. The Giver of all Abundance; the Protector of All Beings; the embodiment of love itself in all its forms. We were one and not one – the paradox that is the mystery of

Eleusis. Persephone lost in the underworld, raped by Hades. Demeter weeping and endlessly searching for her lost child. Myself searching for myself. The world was transformed. All the secular sources in our society of money, of food, of manufacturing, belonged to Her.

And since she and I were one, they belonged to me as well. The bank, the supermarket, General Motors, were all expressions of the endless bounty she produces out of her body – the earth. I sat down on a shelf of bread in the supermarket. Nobody noticed. This was the true bread of life. I mended a broken watermelon, it's red heart bleeding for all the women walking by whose heart's were split in half, exposed and later thrown into the garbage heap. The milk, the sherbet, the ice cream all products from the flesh of cows that were being daily mutilated by unknown forces. In Egypt Hathor was associated with the cow. All the mutilated cows were meant to show us what we were doing. My torso was drawn and quartered – in sympathy with the cows. A balance had to be restored. Everywhere either the pig ruled the day in its greed, its lust, its piggishness alongside the poor mutilated cow lowing in it's pain, giving, giving of it's substance scorned as stupid and positioned with it's udders hooked up to machines. And Demeter weeps and lays waste the land.

She becomes frightened again – resistant at last, perhaps even hopeful. A line from the Homeric Hymn to Demeter becomes a silent mantra "Mother, to you I will tell the whole story exactly and frankly." Not yet. She recounts instead a nightmare: A long corridor made out of a very shiny substance, mirror–like. The dreamer walks down confidently when gradually there is an awareness that what is being reflected on all sides and even above is not a body at all. Merely segments of ears, noses, arms all in frenetic movement. It is in fact not a corridor but a tire tube. There is awful fright and the dreamer tries to find a door to escape. Suddenly these pieces begin to stick to her hands and come off in huge sheets of gluey skin – retaining their resemblance to parts of bodies. After telling this dream she waits for the pain in her stomach to subside. The session ends in a worried silence.

There was never going to be, had been, will have been any way to escape, she realizes now, twisting on the couch, squeezed by words, restrained. The inevitability was acted, prefigured, represented in metaphor, catalogued for future reference.

The morning after what everyone later told me was my assault on the hospital staff, I was removed from the restraints, it was assumed with enough drugs in my system to guarantee my docility.

With nothing on but an open backed hospital gown I decided to escape to a nearby friend's house. I strode out of my room barefoot and proceeded past the nurses' station through the double swinging doors and into the main portion of the hospital. Projecting a strong image of a VISITOR I waited for the elevator but then decided to take the staircase instead. No– one stopped me. I wandered to and fro for some time through the corridors of various wards trying to find the exit and asked an orderly which staircase led outside. He told me. At last I found myself outside the hospital walls in the midst of a scrubby field at the backside of the main building. It didn't seem strange that nothing and no–one had interfered with my escape. I had at last understood something about the power of authority – the authority of power.

A man in a car appeared as I was making my way across a field and offered a lift. I accepted and realized too late that he was from the hospital. The restraints were waiting again and I promised to be good. The Inquisition was simpler in a sense. Poor Giordano knew they were after him and when they caught him he had an opportunity to recant which he declined, choosing instead to make an impassioned speech on his own behalf. In the hours before the authorities arrived to take me to the hospital I attempted to get away with as much intact as possible. By the time the sirens invaded my street, my bones and flesh seemed like a great deal. No time for speeches or heroics. An inelegant escape at best. All in all I'd rather have been Giordano Bruno.

FOUR

SHE IS AWARE THAT THE past is lurking in the Notes she writes, hiding in the book. She is also aware that the Analyst listens well enough to the jokes, the slips, the associations and to the imaginary history – all edited. She ruminates on the possibility that she is fooling the Analyst after all. The French School says that if an analyst is unaware of the subtle movements of the patient's discourse, then both analyst and patient will become lost in the shadow–real of the Imaginary Order forever chasing the ineffable object of desire. Compulsively, she ransacks notebooks, drawers, file cabinets for the outline of events.

THERE CAN BE NO DESIRE HERE.

Fixated, an object of careful scrutiny by Analyst's Evil Eye atomistically fragmenting her body; gazing at her words which reconstruct, build screens, scenes, conundrums and death by dissolution.

It is impossible, here or elsewhere, to permit a real voice, or to permit Angelica to use her voice. She is alarmed at being a subject, even in a book. In spite of that speaking continues, locked in the spaces of pre–history, still announcing the madness; the story.

Maggie mustn't die. And yet unless Maggie and Angelica recognize Alex; until Jean–Claude's disappearance is grasped –One falls silently off a donkey to plunge two hundred feet into the abyss and the other remains in stasis. If Alex is the evil magician disguised as a prince, than Jean–Claude is the prince-still-to- be in his pre–natal form of simpleton. He still must travel through the dark wood, encounter the wise old one, slay the dragon, rescue the princess and displace the old king. Quite a program.

Poor Jean–Claude, after Maggie's death he vanishes, only to reappear in hippie guise on a postcard from some monument taken by one of those old men who frequent the steps of famous buildings. I abandon him there, wandering alone to pick up Angelica's retreat to Switzerland and teaching small boys. Alex is jet-setting in Rome.

One of the nicest things about being mad was the conviction, strange under the circumstances, that at last I was a subject not an object. At last there was complete freedom from a continuous semi–conscious viewing of myself. To be ineluctably myself – feel no eyes upon me, outside or inside was rapture. There were watchers that had to be expelled, foreign substances that were brought to the surface in the heat of the alchemy. Who had been watching me all along? A Pig.

He appeared on the afternoon of day five. There was a gleaming enormous red and black motorcycle in the parking lot of a large hotel. It was the chariot of Priapus. A Pig Priapus. I mounted it and varoomed away to the realm of Using, of raping, of taking without giving in return. Where to give anything is to lose everything. The power of voraciousness. The rush of destroying. Then in the wake of annihilation the all pervading eye of Big Daddy marking one's personality: assessing the tits the legs the ass the beauty the talent the cleanliness the odors the motherhood the cooking the normalcy the conformity the opinions the softness of the hand the sweetness of the breath – CLOSED.

In the next scene a channel spoke to me in tongues transmitting messages from the Akashic records. I heard the narrative of the beginnings on earth told by angels and the tragic events leading to the current impasse. Bad news. Not only was I delusional but inflated as well. The Jewish mystics have a saying that a person should imagine that in their right hand pocket is a piece of paper that says "for me the world was created" and in their left hand pocket an identical piece of paper with the inscription "I am dust and ashes".

Somewhere along the line of my trajectory the left hand piece of paper vanished. Undeniably I was listing. While I didn't believe that the world had been created for me, I more than entertained the thought that I had been created to save the world. To rescue my world. To clean up the pollution in the lakes, the rivers, the oceans; institute commerce between the mainland and the numerous islands, find places where the endangered species might once again flourish and destroy the tyrants forever. And the Lion will lie down with the Lamb. The first step is to emerge from the underworld. And who knows what's been waiting there for the first signs of life.

She knows she has almost exhausted the telling of the salient points in the manufactured autobiography. Free association requests produce lacunas. Long deadly silences in which the possibility of a word appears.

Quickly something interposes language ––this is what she is saying to the listening ear of the Analyst: The Russians tell a story about a little bird lost in the Siberian wastes, starving to death under a mound of snow. A horse roaming the tundra stops to defecate and picks the spot where the little bird is breathing its last. The sudden warmth revives her and pretty soon she begins to peck and hunt the seeds in the steaming mound. She feels so terrific after this immense good fortune that she starts to chirp and flap her wings. A wolf hearing the sound arrives to investigate and promptly gobbles up the bird. Analyst is quiet after this revelation. Too close, she thinks, now Analyst knows I'm afraid of being gobbled up. The fear troubles her for in the Notes she creates and discovers in unexpected places – the trembling is missing, captured in deafness, isolated in misapprehension. So the voice can only be released in disconnection.

※

The madness revealed that I was no longer an object among other objects to be measured in value against motorcycles, cars, camera equipment, personal freedom or rated on a sliding scale against other women. I was subject. Like Job accosted by the voice in the whirlwind I had to make answer. On a dark night in the bathroom I huffed and puffed and blew the house of Hades down, a furious Persephone and the pomegranate was the fruit born in that rage, growing like Hopi corn six feet high in one night.

I couldn't have done it alone. Maggie was there too contributing her hatred and scorn; Angelica too, stripped naked, defiled, robbed, invaded. The litany of crimes was recited and the judgment tendered. *The wicked shall perish. They shall be cut off.*

Alex suffered a body blow that night. Jean–Claude wandering the world– has a vision. The image is Maggie running eternally from the evil magician, fending him off, deceiving him with a mask hard as nails. Angelica is a bewitched prisoner of the same magician trapped in a black and brooding castle high on a hill at the end of the world. Angelica writes to Alex:

"I see myself in your eye. My hair tumbled, the leaves of a nearby tree shading the left side of my face making my cheekbones higher – eyes amber, the curve of my breasts beneath the white blouse, a hand in a delicate pose. I see myself thus reflected – or I cease to exist at all."

Questioning does exist; the slight movement of a curiosity. Attributes of the mad episode did include will, intention, volition, action – all functions assigned to ego – yet Dr. Feingold described the condition as loss of ego. Now she explains that she is confused; does not know. She almost decides to engage in show and tell during the session, overriding objections. Not ready. Her confusion creates bizarre narratives to explain these words she reads again, this metaphorical madness she is subjected to, she is the subject of, which without knowing the referent fill her with panic. It is at this point that Maggie appears with the myth of her death. Now frozen in the pose of patient on a couch, she writes Maggie's death.

"On the way to a monastery sacredly white in the afternoon Greek sun, with the sea sliding away from the shores of the island Maggie's donkey, the last in the line of five – the fifth being the guide's – loses its footing. Maggie, taken by surprise topples off the donkey's back and down two hundred feet of rocky incline to the sea. The 'accident' is unpunctuated by a sound. Silently she falls, and silently touches ground. Up above, Angelica, Alex, Jean–Claude and the Guide stare down in horror. The homeostasis of the island is broken. The tension released, the Gordian Knot untied. Now anything might happen."

Instantly, in the next sentence, the event is transformed; Maggie's death must not be final. the story must continue without interruption no matter what happens. So she is reborn in Angelica; moved to neutral ground in Switzerland. Away from the dark volatile gods of Greece into an affair with Hans, the baker's son. Switzerland's neutrality encourages Angelica's words:

"I met a boy here. He lives in the next chalet. I was taking one of my long walks, (there are no fierce gods here). It was about seven thirty in the evening and tiny lights appeared on the hillsides. Finding a rising field of hay I sat down and was musing on the order below me. He was walking and had picked up a large branch which he was using as a stick. When he saw me he stopped.

-Gruss Gott.

-Gruss Got, I answered.

He waited, pushing the stick into the soft ground. Then he spoke in French.

-You're the teacher, aren't you.

– Yes.

– You live in the next chalet, Fraulein Zsimmer?

– Yes. I've seen you often…

He reddened abruptly and pushed the stick further into the ground. I thought of Marguerita, of her tenderness that was a thin silver thread. For her, I said.

– Would you like to sit down.

He nodded.

–You write?

I could see his eyes, bright points in the tide of night.

–Not exactly, why?

–Because sometimes I pass the chalet and hear the typewriter. I paint.

Would you sit for me?", he blurts out.

Was it the rose and purple mountain of the island, the colors of the rocks beneath the Mediterranean that he saw – Marguerita's face. So I sat for him. I don't know why it's for Maggie, but it is. Maggie was incapable of relating to someone like Hans. She sits on park benches in the cold of Autumn, feeling chilled to the bone, smoking cigarettes, picking up married men."

The floor, the kitchen table, the desk, pieces of furniture are all littered with writings. Word–fragments of multiplied moments, attempts to create the island book, attempts to distill the madness. Parallel to the disintegration of the autobiography crafted while confronting the ceiling belonging to the Analyst she locates the fright of fashioning characters without a history. Arriving at the sessions becomes an ordeal – the car breaks down, she oversleeps. she forgets. It isn't going anywhere. It's going too deep. She awakes one afternoon with the ratty old woman at her side once more:

the fire was dying   eyes were half closed   the
   old woman moved quickly to throw another log
      on the fire   it blazed awake startling the
   people   i tell this story so we do not sleep this
   night   we must see the morning com
   e   tell us then they said shifting
   their feet   rubbing their eyes   knowing
      she was right   for to   sleep now would
   leave them in darkness too long -   -she
      rummaged in a bag and drew out a pipe filling
      it with aromatic herbs   puffing slowly
      the smoke mingling with the fire she spoke
      the middle twists   many snakes in a
      nest   which the head   which
         the tail   which roundness is whose   fingers
   enmeshed   nerves confused   before
      the sorting there is confusion   first
      the oneness that is two   the coupling that is
   many   love is the shape changer the
   dancer the stillness   the song   and the flute
   we move in mirrors   mirages of flesh in a light
      without brightness   we are the dreamer
   being dreamed   when we touch another we toss
   and turn in our sleep   we   become their
   dreams and resist the revelation of ourselves being
      dreamed   for in that great landscape of fantasy
      rising like a coiled spring from a hidden place
            we are transformed into ourselves

FIVE

PSYCHOLOGICALLY sophisticated, she anticipates the next step in the weekly ritual – a layer below history, the mythic supports of a faltering autobiography.

Nevertheless she is not ready to change the tone of the madness – to bring it into focus; to scrutinize it in Freud's landscape; locate those words as psychical reality. Risking something however seems required, an act of faith. Motives and desire are beyond comprehension, but the dreams of the madness, the fairy tale motifs are extracted from the Notes – ritualistically presented.

In the fairy tale of the goose girl, the handkerchief with the three drops of blood that the mother gives to the princess to protect her is lost in the river. The servant takes the place of the princess and has the magical talking horse beheaded. His head hangs on the gate which the princess, now goose girl, must pass each day. "Ah Falada, if my mother knew my fate her heart would surely break" she sighs. The horse head only stares. The Analyst listens attentively to these hidden revelations. The patient recalls the next section in the Notes but does not speak.

❋

Significantly, during the week heralded by the magical lakes surrounding the country house we had gone to for the weekend, I didn't dream at night. I didn't sleep much either. I heard my name being called often, sometimes in the middle of the night, often during the day. Events had to be made to happen; rituals had to be performed in sequence.

The three drops of blood had to be restored, the heart made whole again. The elements of ritual were always available. On the porch surrounding the house, a guest had left a sewing needle. In full view of several friends, I released the three drops of blood from the large toe, in a prescribed triangular formation. The horse head moans with relief, freed at last from it's bondage. The goose girl becomes the princess again. All things right themselves.

The moment for death and rebirth arrived on Sunday morning. A large oblong hole had been dug under the porch in an attempt to fix some plumbing. I lay in this grave, a pine branch on my chest, eyes closed until I was called forth, Persephone\Artemis to the light of day. Rising from the chthonic depths of Hades to bathe in the river; careening down the steep hillside, leaping over logs, skimming over rocks, Artemis awoke. Heaven and earth were reunited in a mysterium of nature in which I was the root, the tree, the branch the leaves the flower and fruit. The sacrifice of the three drops of blood summoned the Virgin Goddess with her arrows of vengeance. My right arm could be raised; my refusal developed hands and feet. At last I lived in constant protection, within the abiding grace and abundance of Demeter.

❋

She ponders the hieroglyphics of her utterances to the Analyst. She ponders herself in the past/present madness, in the Notes as well as the resilience of the characters in the island book. Janus faced Angelica or Maggie – invent contingent freedoms– qualified resistance. Angelica impresses herself with a moment with Alex.

"That last day. Oddly gray, turning cold, the olive trees naked, the rocks without sun – a moon landscape, uninviting, harsh. I see my hand silhouetted against the tree, falling, an immense rock toward you. Your face immobile, your eyes watching me. A crack, like ice, like branches breaking in winter. Your face turning red in an instant. You blinked. I can still feel my hand burning in my pocket, some fantastic torch, still hear the ocean grumbling in the distance; feel the small stones scurrying underfoot."

After attributing that slap to Angelica's new found freedom, a seeming gift from Alex, she writes that as he turned away, he had a slight smile on his face. Almost immediately following this event Maggie dies, the island is abandoned and the three remaining characters are dispersed. Retribution. Angelica delivers a richly deserved slap to Alex and she's banished to Switzerland with the added penance of exonerating him through her abiding and unfaltering love.

Shockingly the Stone suffers a transfiguration. No longer an absent presence menacing in its speechless solidity, something to be overcome, it now possesses a perilous softness. She worries about this event, devises schemes and finally abandons the idea of risk. She is infuriated by this cowardice, by terrors, by a bone–cracking weakness on this couch/platform of performance, this stage–fright. Resistant to the inevitable continuation of the madness story insisting on unfolding.

❋

When the three ambulance guards arrived –afraid to get too close –I begged them not to take me. I could hear the ambulance siren. Then it suddenly became clear to me that I was to be sacrificed. That like Osiris, I was to be cut into fourteen pieces, roasted on the barbecue and a new twist, cannibalistically consumed. Unlike those shamans happily submitting to dismemberment; their bones removed one by one, cleaned out and replaced with gems, their flesh cut off, their arms and legs thrown into the fire – I refused. I fought like a demon with a faint heart. For, although I couldn't trust anyone – above, below or in the middle realms –a terrible question arose – a giant koan ascending with me inside it and mercifully I fainted.

These angry terrors invaded in spite of the fact that I had been abundantly presented with a vision of perfect safety. Perhaps because of that vision Angelica never experiences the terror that walks by day, night sweats, dismemberment. She lives in the constant illusion of Alex's love, forever in potentia. Perhaps then it is she, not Maggie at all, who is dancing to the beat of the patriarchal drum. Maggie is deaf. When her ears finally open all sounds for a time are chaos. So Angelica struggles to maintain her relationship with Alex while experiencing Maggie as a ghostly geis. Still, she must know that she cannot remain in Switzerland/ neutral land forever producing fragments of phrases.

She must know since she writes: "Switzerland is beginning to suffocate me. The relentless geraniums, the mountains an ever present passive backdrop – cyclorama worthy of more than rows of neat houses, restaurants and tourists all year round. The Swiss allow themselves to go mad only once a year on top of a mountain, beside a raging bonfire. It's time to go forward or rather back." Angelica has received several postcards from Jean–Claude, at this point the messages have no significance. The obligation is clear. Amerika looms. Both home and exile. Angelica is the seed. She will carry the postcards, Maggie's wandering spirit, the diaries written to Alex, past the immigration officials in New York City.

The dyad is approaching a threshold –the Analyst is alert; the patient casts around for metaphors to deflect the reality of a narrative. Although she admits herself to the space in the ceiling, a growing dimension of words becoming flesh, the mirror–image of the masked biography remains in place. Nevertheless, she is anxiously aware that pressure is mounting. The mirror will crack exposing the madness, recapitulating the past, inscribing the mirror with acid.

She pauses to rest and discovers Derrida saying Freud: "They [the dream symbols] frequently have more than one or even several meanings, and, as with Chinese script, the correct interpretation can only be arrived at on each occasion from the context."

This she imagines is a clue about decoding. Additionally, she observes that as the shadows on the ceiling created with words take shape, the idea of a bridge to writing appears spontaneously.

SIX

RESIGNATION SUPERVENES. The language of the sessions is shifting. She constructs or deconstructs herself, unsure of which it is as she fades trapped in the fabrication of the madness, of collecting the data. She can only trust in the Analyst's metal file cabinet now since the biography will be reaching a terminus – a threshold. Everybody needs a biography in America.

Some of the time she exists before the madness, then after it's advent, here traveling backwards or catapulted forward to a point beyond the revelations. Pinned in the relentless movement, the insistence of a record, of coding, of transcription. She must attend, is captivated by time ripping itself out. She no longer knows if Analyst hears this being spoken, or if the words are only part of the book writing itself.

❋

Traffic between the denizens of the underworld and the Gods of Olympus has been steady. Zeus asks Hades carefully, apologetically to reconsider the abduction of Persephone. He asks so politely that Hades sees his advantage and refuses. Olympus was more familiar than my own masked face. On the way back from that fateful weekend four of us were sitting in the front of the truck and as I gazed out of the window the heavens opened. The clouds formed again and yet again the resplendent faces forms and vehicles of Olympus. There, to my left was Zeus, his muscles rippling around one of the many nymphs he ravished, his curly beard grazing her cheek. The face of Hermes obscured by light, lounged to the left of his father. Then Olympus itself was revealed with Demeter, Persephone and Triptolemus – the Great Mother bearing aloft the sacred wheat, the daughter and mother one in a mysterious symbiosis. They saved the best for last – bearing down on us all from the right, riding a chariot led by six solar horses Apollo in a blaze of glorious sunshine, his hair streaming, his mighty arms holding the reins, racing across the late afternoon sky.

Angelica returning to New York writes :

"Memory fades, dreams die, Gods vanish. Sometimes you have to beat the ground with sticks, tap out rhythms, still it might not rain. Gods are capricious here. Everybody needs a biography in Amerika. It is a decree. Archetypes shrink, meanings change."

So, the obligation is clear: fabricate biographies for the characters. Here is Maggie in New York.

Subject: Marguerita (Maggie) Fox

Small frame, fair hair, below average height. A dark skin with large eyes that move from yellow to green. The family joked about her appearance attributing the fair hair and light eyes to a sudden influx of foreign genes – an ancient rape.

Henry Fox, the father, was a salesman traveling the Northeast region with boxes and racks of shirts which his charming and extroverted personality turned into desirable items for the populations of a series of small out of the way towns cut off from the mainstream. He found her mother sequestered and fading behind the counter of one of the shops in one of these towns. No one had ever joked with her before – not like Henry did – not with the suggestion of forbidden pleasures in his laugh. Her name was Anna and her mother was watchful but busy and Anna became pregnant. At first she wouldn't tell. Henry wasn't due back in town for another two months and had no notion of what the angry fates had planned. Anna's mother browbeat her into confessing, bought two tickets to New York and pounced on Henry dragging her only mildly resisting daughter. She was awesome. Henry did the right thing.

Maggie was born seven and a half months later. Anna's mother insisted that family life would change Henry. It didn't. He stayed away longer and longer on his selling trips. His wife received phone calls from women, drunk and laughing, until Henry would get on the phone explaining that he was at a shirt fair and that's the way they always were. Anna could understand. She thought, had been told, she was dull and plain, couldn't cook, was an indifferent housekeeper was shy and frightened of everything. Her mother kept telling her that if she were a different sort of woman she could get Henry in line. On top of that, she couldn't take care of Maggie. Maggie alarmed her. It was a source of continuous wonderment that Maggie was flesh of her flesh. Maggie never talked about Henry and ran off with an Italian drummer in a rock band when she was sixteen. She kept away from all of them.

Even in New York, the reduced, modified, masked Marguerita Fox has an advantage over Angelica. She has a profession. Angelica just grew. She has no past, no future, no biography, no profession. She drifts. Obsessively waiting. Unwilling to even leave New York, it was Maggie who initiated the trip to Greece, Maggie that picked up Alex on the island, Maggie that in fact found the island and Jean–Claude as well.

Here's Jean–Claude diminished in New York:

Subject: Jean–Claude Viale

Average height, brown hair, light eyes, mesomorphic. A distinguishing feature is the nose, which is rather too large giving the eyes a small sad look. The father is French, the mother American. They met when she went to study art in Paris long after the war. He liked her natural American optimism, her enthusiasm, and a kind of general merriness that was in very short supply in post–war Paris. They had a passionate love affair that made them both feel guilty and resolved the guilt by getting married.

Afterward, they spent their time jogging back and forth between Paris and Connecticut working up a nice paper import business (with the help of her father). Regine was the first and then Jean–Claude and Sissy (otherwise known as Madeleine) who were twins – a surprise that arrived from her side of the family. Jean–Claude's childhood was singular by reason of its general good humor, uneventfulness and closeness to Sissy. In typical fashion he wandered into marriage with one of Sissy's roommates at College. A woman who fit so well into the family there was hardly a bump when they set up house in a small New York apartment while he pursued the paper business and she learnt film editing. Their little bark might have meandered in the shallows had it not been for an unpremeditated walk in Central Park in October.

There is more. What he said to Maggie sitting on a bench with one glove on, the other hand naked and chilled holding a cigarette. "May I sit down?" Although what prompted that forever remains a mystery. And more. What Maggie said: "It's a free country." When he asked if he could see her again, after coffee and some talk in a nearby restaurant "If you want." And later: "Don't get divorced on account of me JC". And so on.

She muses on these biographies, products of an attempt to fill in the blanks – the empty pasts of the characters – is amused by their opacity. She is aware of the failure to replicate that opaqueness for herself for the benefit of Analyst. Or does she succeed in fact and when a sufficient and necessary quantity of words will have been accumulated both she and Analyst will at last be inundated and fall through the center of the earth.

She ponders that all this anxiety, encouraged by the process in the Analyst's office has no meaning on New York island separated from the mainland of Amerika. There, Maggie re–creates herself each day, each hour, a contingent existence depending on variables of uptown, downtown, French cafes, dress shops, book stores, bus stops. Constant movement a cataract of bodies, faces familiar as comforting others – all that structures a floating symbolic language of selfness. When exhaustion sets in she sleeps in the apartment she shares with Angelica – sometimes for days– dreaming. In this way she dreamed the trip to Greece for both of them.

She reluctantly admits to herself that this "talking cure" is affecting changes in writing –causing it to move out of stasis, out of mere letters, into sentences, paragraphs – nevertheless she clings to the false biographies written to appease. She continues to pretend that this "talking cure" involves the breakdown alone – the experience in the hospital, the preamble of madness performed without fear. So she continues to find, edit, re–write, remember. But before she consents to know that she might be speaking out loud to the ceiling about the madness; before she submits to undergo the fear of exposure, of descent, she returns to the book and finds:

Jean–Claude is actually half French, however Alex bears the name French. And language conveys vitally important messages, carries much more than imagined. I changed my name two or three times during the implosion shifting middle name to first, erasing last name altogether.

Alex French is not French. Jean–Claude – – now that he is at last lost, bedraggled and sick with love his life in New York shrivels to a paper cut out and blows out to sea. Alex never inhabits New York at all.

Creativity on the couch, she thinks. Words to fill Analyst's file folder. A construction of a life that slips constantly at first in the office then elsewhere. Biography fills the gaps, seals the entrances, but appears to be more effective when surrounded by a vague silence. This "talking cure" might in fact be a word–shredder after all. Relentlessly she persists in staging the past. Biography as caulking.

Subject: Alex French

Above average height, brachcephalic skull, dark hair light eyes and fair skin that resists tanning. His mother was small, vivacious, had wanted to be an actress. She always retained the habit of nervously watching other people react to her behavior seeking approval, a trait her son detested, along with her secret drinking which everyone knew about. His father was lanky, taciturn and liked to fish. He would take Alex and his younger brother Robert on long fishing trips to which the mother was never invited. The "boys" maintained that her chatter and perpetual jerky movements to fetch things from baskets drove the fish away.

Early on he discovered the worlds that sand could create and later, disgusted with the imperfect ability of the material, the persistent attacks by the ocean, he switched to clay, modeling city after city, expanding them on a card table his own private domain. Robert had dared once to touch the towering buildings, escaping certain death through the intervention of his father, who although he saved poor Robert's skin, tacitly agreed with Alex. His world contained dwellings of all kinds, parks, theaters, mountains in the distance trees, flowers, shrubs, rocks and rivers. Hours would be expended finding just the right placement for a bench so that the imagined patrons of the park could have the best view.

Architecture was the obvious choice.

The card table grew and became sites. Ideas and principles were translated into brick and mortar, the purity of space prevailed, people were merely objects inhabiting sacred space. And during the madness the inner location which was responsible for Alex became psychotic. The house became the focal point for cosmic battles: it had to be protected from attack with rocks and stones, sticks and crosses, grates and bones, candles and books, arranged in perfect order. Nothing could be left out, nothing overlooked.

She grasps at last that a catastrophe is imminent. A disaster is bound to break through all the silly biographies, all the plaster. Does the genesis of the characters have anything to do with these falsifications; did they always truly reside on the island in Greece where their story keeps trying to begin? Jean–Claude wanders in angst and love while Angelica continually transcends.

Up, up, up she goes, higher and higher until from that lofty perch all objects merge and blend, all life itself is panorama. Unlikely though it may seem, up there at the top is a transmogrified, transformed, resurrected Alex. Down below, where she never ventures willingly, where the darkness is great, lives the other face of that same Alex. In middle–earth, a wasteland there is Hans and postcards from Jean–Claude. And Maggie's ghost provides a voice in the Notes left behind which Angelica reads gingerly, guiltily in the middle of the night.

"No amount of thinking can ever determine our actions. Our real actions are conceived in darkness, in the womb of time and are born howling into the moment."

Abruptly she loses confidence in the translation of experience into this process – the trembling returns, the fears ignite again, more sharply than at first. The space is suffocating, too hot even dangerously overheated. Chillingly the language that speaks her describes the body as the field of disaster. Descent is inevitable.

Now the story can begin:

Once upon a time, far, far away, beyond the seven seas and even further, there lived behind the crumbling walls of a ramshackle oven, in the seventy seventh fold of an old woman's skirt, a white flea and in the very middle of its belly there was an island.

Two beautiful princesses lived on the island. One was fair, the other dark; they were like night and day. When they were very small, the Queen went away to visit her sisters in a far off land. While she was gone the King who was an evil magician contrived to murder the two little girls. A good fairy godmother put the little girls in caskets and set them adrift in the ocean to protect them from the magic of their wicked father. The sea nurtured them and the cave spirits sheltered them until they were grown. They knew nothing of their origins or the inheritance of the rich kingdom that was rightfully theirs.

The white flea is compelled to move and New York comes into view. Ultimately in spite of biographies, banalities, conditioning, medication, exorcism, Angelica will arrive back in New York with her luggage heavier by one white flea.

SEVEN

BIOGRAPHY, AUTO speak has come to its inevitable end. Now, a different level of anxiety is manifested – the anxiety of disaster, of a fall into catastrophe. She attempts to explain speaking in language culled from secret readings out of analysis school: "what seems to be first.... is the anguish of the corps morcele". The corps morcele is a term for a violently nontotalized body image, an image psychoanalysis finds accompanied by anxiety. The mirror stage is a decisive moment. Not only does the self issue from it, but so does the body in bits and pieces. The anguish of the body in bits and pieces.

She finds confirmation for that in attending to the utterances, the pictographs prefigured in the ruins of the madness.

❋

Ragged disenfranchised soldiers, one night of the year, amid feasting and reveling in the streets of Rome, were permitted entrance to the sacred honor of becoming priests of Cybele. As the night wore on, each soldier would pick out the house of a rich man then the soldier would cut his penis off and throw it through the window. The owner of the house was then obliged to bring in the castrato, succor him, dress him in elegant women's attire and in several weeks present him as a neophyte at the temple of Cybele.

Origen castrated himself for the love of God.

Abelard was castrated by his uncle–Father in law for the love of Heloise. Cronus, the youngest of the Titan sons of Uranus, armed with a sickle castrated his father during the rebellion of those in Tartarus. From the wound, three drops of blood fell to earth and produced the Furies, while the genitals themselves that Cronus had cast into the sea, in foamy confusion, yielded up Aphrodite. The Goddess of Love.

On one of the worst days preceding the hospitalization, I was fully convinced that a terrible mutilating operation had been performed on my urethra under the pretense of having my tonsils removed when I was five. Castration was a reality.

The earth's axis shifted, darkness and light, male and female, the sun and the moon, all polarities rotated one hundred eighty degrees and back again in a dizzying sequential gyration. The polar ice caps melted and the waters covered the earth.

Leviathan roams in those seas. Up above the swirling waves the ragged wings of the Erinyes hiss in the wind. Lost is the panoramic cloud vision of the Gods of Olympus. the Titans reign. In spite of the nativity of Aphrodite, Cronus follows his father and swallows his own children until the stony dinner given him by Rhea to save the life of Zeus. And it is only when it will come to pass that Cronus himself is depotentiated by a thunderbolt and banished to Tartarus that the Goddess of Love can freely harass Olympians and mortals.

※

She denies the last two sessions with their anxiety. And instead this paid–for safety of the couch, of the silence of her own voice skirting words, seems flimsy. Much too fragile to contain these volatile bits and pieces of body/ego. She contemplates quitting. Yet, somehow, as full of holes as it is, the container still holds. Quitting is impossible at this point. She recognizes the feeling –vaguely–a memory of the terror of loving, perhaps a fragment from the book.

Angelica writes to Alex:

"So love again, a fantastic detour.

It was all a love story after all. The distillation of all our efforts at philosophy. You think you were immune, like Spiros and Georgos. Spiros was the one, very tall quite thin, with masses of grey and black hair, a natty dresser. He owned the taverna, while Georgos was short and plump, always on some secret business in Athens. While we struggled in the glue of time and love, moving in slow motion, they whirled around us picking off English and American tourists like ducks in a shooting gallery. And as we ever moved more slowly, the world seemed to vanish."

To intervene, to prescribe, Analyst suggests the writing of a story. She makes up many utilizing stock images, then reluctantly, hesitantly, certain of doom, she retrieves the story embedded in the book. First, alone she threads it to the hospital bed in translation. Through a small aperture she sees: That while she lay there, helpless, knowing with the certitude that terror brings, that the dragon was flying toward her. That though she hoped it was one of those paper dragons that dance along the streets at Chinese New Year, filled with laughing faces of friends and neighbors, at the same time its dreadful wings were too loud, that the laughing faces would in a moment transform themselves into grinning demons. At about four o'clock in the morning the truth dawned – the evil magician was Janus faced and terrible.

In this way she is enabled to continue the story of the evil magician and the princesses:

Many years later, the evil magician found out that the two little princesses were alive. That he had been fooled with the hearts of some rabbits. Further, that now, at last, there was a righteous young man in the land who had been overheard in a tavern decrying these evil deeds. who had vowed to restore the young princesses to their rightful inheritance. Through the offices of his fearful necromancy, he had the young man castrated by the inhabitants of that underworld whom he forced to his will. With the severed organ he made a homunculus, which permitted him access to the hero's form and face whenever he wished. The powerful three drops of blood that had fallen from the wound, he kept in a small vial, well guarded by night creatures, and he banished the young man to the ends of the earth.

Among Maggie's papers Angelica finds another piece which signals change.

"The harbor gleams brightly in the sun, small boats, a flock of birds, mountains, three cats dozing on the pier. The two suitcases weigh heavily. No porters. Again something ludicrous, a mockery in all this luggage, at this time, standing here with Jean–Claude's letter, still and white in my hand, a dead bird. He asks me why I run and I have no answer.

"The sun is an orange dripping. The silence of heat. Everything gently baking in white and gold. Through the steaming haze, ocher blue flesh of sea sleeping motionless, the skin of a fabulous fruit. The sound of a jet collapses on the harbor."

EIGHT

SHE FEELS MUCH stronger; a strength tempered by wary cleverness. Occasionally she will speak a language of myths without characters. The words still refuse to enter, have no proper names. She imagines a diagnosis of this phase in the analysis She dreams what Analyst might say: At this point we have a condition. Clinically, this could be schizoid fragmentation, demonstrating the ambivalence of a center that cannot hold. But mythically, we can discern a god in the disease.. Schizoid Polycentricity is a style of consciousness and not only a disease, and it likes plural meanings, cryptic double–talk and psychically detached and separated body parts. She is dubious about the usefulness of signaling to Analyst that speech is near, because she feels memory, re-membering throbbing in her chest. She also is able to read that other utterance, that performance which Analyst must only guess at; merely analyze.

Hermes was born on the weekend of Eleusis. Usually he was a strand of wayward hair. He's tricky and whimsical, laughable and winsome. It is hard to remember he's a God after all. Magic, at least Hermes magic is an expression of love. A mere twist of my hair, and I was informed of what kind of ritual would right some wrong, replace something lost, and with the help of the great thief himself, whose first act was to steal Apollo's cows, we would chase down, capture and destroy psychic thieves and force them to return their ill gotten gains. Hermes is the guide of souls; a guide that echoes the type of guidance accorded the blind Zen master by one of his students who led him directly into a brick wall. The old Zen teacher mutters, thank you, thank you. What trust is evidenced here in the creaky, unhinged workings of the world.

❋

She recognizes that a belief in the analysis, despite herself, is emerging. Immediately she discovers a preference – to forget the sessions, the weekly grinding, the confrontations with potential losses –so many that they have congealed into a solid lump. This Analyst has become important after all. Too important. Something is coming in –, which signifies something will go out. She refuses to connect the progress of the book, of writing with the Analyst, with the couch, a bed of nails which constantly threatens to become an embrace. Regardless of the logic of choices, she is compelled to continue with the book, the narrative plunging on: The center cannot hold. The island erupts into fragments.

Jean–Claude is eating vegetables and doing yoga in India, while Angelica, will arrive at any moment in Kennedy airport without an apartment, a job, money, and will burst into tears when Mr. Gianelli (his tag identifies him) says cheerily, "Hey, welcome home, you've been gone a long time." Presently she is a perfect target: serious, frightened, carrying her restless Maggie ghost, her pathetic lovesick projections onto Alex, her letters that never arrive at any destination.

"There's no point in repudiating the letters although now they seem absurd, our whole non– existent relationship even more absurd. How could I not have seen in my struggles to make sense out of everything that happened, of you, especially of you, the dreams created to find myself. In any case, to find myself is an expression of another myth. In retrospect, your potential frown obscured a good portion of the summer sky of Greece and often I found myself dancing to the tune your vengeful puppet gods sang."

In the early morning, she is sitting up in bed, alarmed by an elusive image, the pad by the bed flies into her hand, the pen poised for the rush of unwitting words; writing as portent. Angelica is verging on the truth that Alex's sacred space is very small and Maggie's wild gyrations offend and upset him. He will play her game long enough to gain an advantage; then he will excoriate the game, call it quits, rip up the board and whip out his blueprints. And that slap that Angelica delivered in the wake of suspecting this truth, although he smiled out of habit, had more effect than she supposed.

And now, Angelica, released from the turgid air of Europe, gliding along at 600 miles an hour and is about to land in the Zone of Mercury in the midst of the swirling waves. Descending into the city of lies, of superfluities, of fake biographies, of subway sea creatures, of layers of reality she reads about Heloise and Abelard. She reads of love that continues on broken, castrated. Does the book stop here? Does the writing stop at the point when she who is writing realizes that she wrote Angelica reading the book she herself wanted to read - her dream of Heloise and

Abelard . No, nothing stops, she thinks, She persists in producing scraps of paper, words without a home, still flying, still landing, still writing more words to Alex, her face veiled:

"Maybe you knew all along that sooner or later the four of us who took part in that summer would have to finally commit to paper and behind the scenes reveal a face, a truer face perhaps." Angelica writes.

And there is an obsession with masks. It's one of the few objects she can collect, does not lose. African, Indian, Asian and as a logical extension puppets, dolls and even Maggie with her acting; the mercurial nature of relationships, the prevarication, all collectibles. Time and again in the letters she attempts to force Alex to reveal himself; to take off his mask. The identical compulsion manifests towards Maggie.

"I was surprised when one morning I went into her room to get something and found Maggie asleep, fully clothed, white socks, jeans and a yellow sweater that once had been mine. Over it another bulkier sweater in blue and green, one arm across her face.

She had left one side of the shutters open and hot yellow specks of dust slid into the room spotlighting one hand drifting over the end of the bed; over the red and purple rug with a package of Pallas, unopened. I could ask why I see that tableau new minted each time and yet when I try to conjure Maggie, the image remains shattered mirror under water fragmenting away into darkness."

Predictably it seems Jean–Claude is not required to make revelations. And Angelica herself has slipped through so far, commenting, talking about, but she is seen even as she sees. I can see her face in the window, dreaming of death in love, of black and red, of mandalas, high above the polluted air of New York.

With her waist length black braid resting on her right shoulder, looping over her breast and barely touching pages of the opened book; her dark eyes closed against the hum of the airplane; she thinks, rather imagines an exegesis on love, the myth of saving bastards.

Meanwhile, offstage, Hermes the messenger of the Gods who promised his father that he wouldn't tell lies but could not always tell the whole truth, implies, hides, and never reveals the alarming truth that the Gods, having been somewhat demoted to archetypes, are really congenital transvestites, engaging in a dazzling dance of mutual love–making and baroque castrations.

In spite of that, Angelica ponders a final resolution, an ultimate revelation of the truth chasing Alex's imago through a maze, armed with love and little else, hoping for the critical moment of transformation. So she persists in forgetting that in spite of the love and noble love letters of Heloise to Abelard medieval history gains more than these lovers perpetually separated, not in a fairy tale, but in the sad truth of reality of the time. Heloise as the "devil's door".

Poor Heloise. Poor Angelica.

The design and purport of the letters to Alex to effect a reversal; to shower enough kisses on the beast until the denouement–transformation into the beloved image; the image held all along in spite of any action that belied it; every defect, all signs and signals of error. If Angelica sets herself up as the modern Heloise attempting a remodeling of Alex through a combination of insight via words and faultless love, then her obfuscation of herself must be a symptom, a disease, a God.

Maggie's eternal dying without death reverberates in Angelica's eternal loving without issue, stillborn in an irreconcilable fiction. And we have Angelica: elusive, masquerading behind the scrim of men's dreams of perfecting themselves, their art, through the personal presence of a woman, no longer remaining anonymous. As much as she is Maggie's sister, she is mine as well, though that's an association I would rather avoid. It must be said, otherwise it will never be written:

We are connected at the spinal cord, back to back, like the two boys in the old school rhyme. "One fine day in the middle of the night two dead boys got up to fight, back to back they faced each other, drew their swords and shot each other."

NINE

THE COUCH IS A bed of nails. The silence demands an answer, an utterance. Her tears fall into her hair, spread out on a blue cushion. All lies she thinks, all a waste of money, of time. This space colluded with a presence grown familiar, even loved, to elicit only daylight words. The trajectory has already been mapped, she thinks, long ago at the appearance of the first letter, the singular word. She is only able to hope that, after all the talking, she will still remain as she relinquishes, backs off, retreats.

Madness and/or fiction as myth, as metaphor, as symbolic representation, as vision, as journey, as distortion as sickness and none of these or all of them produces a potion of the underworld that must never be drunk. Dark shoots of memory.

Therefore, at last, at Note nine. the last unitary number, the solitary number related to one, the beginning and the end, it must be said that, yes, it is true that the characters in the book stand sentinel to uninvestigated, forgotten rooms in the house of psyche. Somewhere along the line of creating its prophetic incidents failures grief and fantasies I considered that if I could dispense with Maggie everything would be fine. The room to which she holds the key would remain forever sealed. But Maggie will not die. And now Angelica will not accept her role as Heloise to Alex's definitely uncastrated, never castrated at all, Abelard.

As long as we emulate the three headed Cerberus the gate to Hades in locked and unseen. At night the three heads talk to each other, tell each other distracting tales. Their faces are hidden from each other, but their voices are heard in obscurity. When shall we three meet again, in thunder, lightning or in rain. Then a cryptic message, a warning.

Somewhere near the beginning Angelica writes, Cassandra like –"–We don't know ourselves well enough to predict which rocketing event will finally cave in our precarious orbits."

Does Angelica, safe in the citadels of Olympus know that soon, soon the flaming sword will cease its gyrations, the three heads of Cerberus will merge and heaven/hell will become realities?

And what of the ratty old lady, so long silent?
Oh she sits now in a glade alone her back
against a small scrubby tree listening to a river
invisible on the left   So the sea must be near
there is no fire this time   no campsite   only
the sun brightly alert casting shadows of
grass   her eyes are closed and she mumbles
to   herself   this is the moment in the
story when the tiger stirs   the snakes   uncoil
this is no resting place this is the place of advent
now amidst the rubble is a death head with pearls

in its eye sockets   death with life unborn in its
mouth   now I shall have to   move so
the story can tell itself   now the people will
have to   weep and tear their clothes and rub ashes
into their faces   put out   the fire
and eat the darkness

TEN

SHE CONSIDERS A WORD: Kinship.

Angelica is airborne, the oxygen diminishing, the plane on fire. Changes have opened the circles enough to cancel the monumental spacecraft. Mutable lines and the plane drops out of the sky. She speculates as she falls into the couch, as she pulls the cover closer, on what Analyst is imagining.

"Memory not only records it also confabulates, that is it makes up imaginary happenings, wholly psychic events. Memory is a form imagination can borrow in order to make its personified images feel utterly real. Because we experience these events in the 'past' we believe they really happened as facts."

She fervently hopes this is so. But instead when the non–memories arrive as the plane is descending she ceases to exist, becomes a non–self with a no–fact recollection – a forgotten reverie. Angelica, Maggie, Alex, Jean–Claude with all their signs symbols modifiers trailing their significations –this text as mirror fades.

Before this word appeared – this word kinship–the interpretation of these Notes, this text, this non–

analysis could proceed empirically, directed at a patient on a couch – an empirical accident. After this word kinship no–one is here – in fact the session has fallen into a black hole – the anti–universe of discourse. Here as has already been told the sun and the moon are indistinguishable.

And here in the crepuscular light there is a child. She is running. Running away in a small living room with blue furniture. She wears a yellow sun suit (it must be summer then you say). She is two and half. The strap of her yellow sun suit has been torn and dangles behind her disconnected. The left front of the bib is folded down helplessly. Soon the shadow will catch her. Soon the sun suit will be taken off. Soon the roaring will begin. Her chubby legs circle in a closed space. Soon the smells will begin; soon the terror will swallow the world.

Maggie smiles in her mock–grave; she sees the key turning in the lock.

ELEVEN

NOW THAT THE WRITING has come to a standstill, the last shield has disintegrated in exhaustion. She knows that no–one is there to listen. No dreams arrive to elaborate the voiceless monologue of the sessions; she remembers at last that everything has been forgotten...all things, objects, people, gone in fact, never part of a narrative, leaving only traces, a sad spoor. She sinks, vanishes into a no–land of depression, a wasteland – wasted–land. The pictures keep coming, badly cut film; jumpy, disconnected –but she knows she must find the words or her body will shatter into a thousand pieces. Yet nothing will die finally. The words continue, Angelica continues, Maggie persists, and the men travel. The Notes arrive.

Nothing ever occurs there in the circle of revelations. She imagines nothing but sound, cogent sound. She's not alone; there is always the sense of another, an Other. Alone, the body volcanically erupts forth its secret knowings, who then witnesses for these syllables?

She wakes up groping darkly to the dreaded bathroom, a space never seen, never to be seen ever again as real space. First it is as always unnoticed, imagined from pictures in magazines, utilitarian. Then there is a glimpse of the feet of a bathtub a tile floor, whitened one inch tiles, blackened grout cold on the back, legs still chubby, adrift in the air somewhere down there, floating away into brightness – something is happening (what?) down there. Something forgotten forever. Even so, the body remembers, the cells shriek, the pain doubles her over into the silence of a toilet bowl.

She will not lie down again on the friendly couch, won't tell, will tell, won't tell, will tell. Won't write, will write. Is this an autobiography?

TWELVE

WHEN THE BOOK SURFACES in the crevices of the real world she believes that Angelica is writing the Notes. From time to time, seeking a respite she carts them to that Other, allows them to be part of a story collecting in the locked file of another place.

I made twenty or thirty phone calls from the hospital and wrote the telephone numbers of my friends relatives doctors in different colors in my address book. Much later when I looked through it the numbers would appear written in black or red, crosswise on the page or sometimes upside down. A way of defining myself – a way of cataloguing change?

The trouble with madness is that it is not neat. At least from the inside it isn't. The world of light without shadow, run as the Australian aborigines say, by the people who have eyes but can't see, creates order, system, labels, even Gods who now are diseases. But in the chthonic depths, once the potion is consumed only shadowy motion, moonlight demons, and transformations exist. All Gods are there mingling, marrying, differentiated only momentarily, then their faces melt and change.

Uncle Lack–Limb and Uncle Lame–Gait were seeing the sights at Dark Lord Hill and the wastes of K'un– lun, the place where the Yellow Emperor rested. Suddenly a willow sprouted out of Uncle Lame–Gait's left elbow. He looked very startled and seemed to be annoyed. "Do you resent it" said Uncle Lack Limb. "No, what is there to resent", said Uncle Lame Gait. "To live is to borrow. and if we borrow to live, then life must be a pile of trash. Life and death are day and night. You and I came to watch the process of change and now change has caught up with me. Why would I have anything to resent?"

❋

She realizes that Analyst remarks the lack of affect in the selected episodes of the madness. Wonders how they connect, where they fit in the narrative. She escapes often to Angelica's interrupted musings on the island, on the drama taking place there in a mist cast up by the hot boiling sea.

Once there were four people on an island.

One had been a voyager in a small sturdy boat, unaware of the vastness of the sea, caught in the net of himself, which he thought he had cast overboard.

One had been shipwrecked far out to sea and swam ashore singing a lonesome doomed song.

One sat for years on the sandy banks of another sea and sent messages in bottles. They all returned unopened forcing him finally to get up and try in person.

One had developed a passion for the endless sea–light, but was night–blind.

They were each other's dreams.

THIRTEEN

LIVING IS A NIGHTMARE. Suddenly the nausea would come or a blinding headache signaling body speech. And these events, irresistible, compelling the re–enactment of suffering, could never be reduced to words – remained a mute residue which she sometimes attempted to articulate in the office of silence, the room of double speech. She was always disappointed, always bereft, as the words, so carefully chosen dragged experience into the file, into a case history, into another statistic.

This is all too confused, too fragmented; she hears these words being spoken to a woman, a rather interesting looking woman, vacantly attentive behind her. The book is the most important priority, isn't it? Isn't that why she began this interminable process? She objects to the cessation of her everyday life. She had such a life once. She dimly realizes that she is angry. Mad at Maggie for dying. Maybe Alex killed her after all? Maybe it wasn't an accident or suicide. Ahh – a sentence arrives through the air – the Sphinx like Analyst formulates a question –

Who is Maggie for you?

The question frightens her, opens the abyss. Quickly she will change all their names – except Maggie's. Angelica will be Molly, Alex will be Paul. In a fury she insists on giving them the kind of attitudes, of reactions she imagines she missed and wishes she could have had.

❀

The wind was ferocious and the long walk from the plane to the terminal doors blew the scene, the script from her mind, leaving her to rely solely on a vague, oceanic movement in the region of the solar plexus.

He emerged from a welter of pastel pantsuits and polyester leisure suits punctuated by an occasional bolo tie, cowboy hat and jeans. Hair grown back – a black halo – he hugged her quickly, too quickly so she couldn't see his face in that first moment and hustled down to pick up the luggage, keeping up an excited conversation about New York. Determined to reenact an old football weekend. To pretend Greece never happened.

Airports are collective places, evoke general images and personas. Some opened out into nowhere, suspending place, allowing anything to happen. This one was too diminutive, too concerned with presenting an interesting entry into the Southwest. So when he saw that she wasn't going to play the game of the All–American girl, he lapsed into a sullen silence.

The car rolled down the highway, struggling up impossible hills. Mountains, scrub desert, unrealistic blue sky. Buttes suddenly looming up in tawny colors imitating shapes of animals, faces of long dead and forgotten Gods, scattered about as if thrown by an angry hand. This place was old. Older than Greece. An irony that it should be in the New World. Maybe something might be salvaged before the silence defeated them both. She sank into the seat and took a quick breath.

- Paul .. She paused to let the tone of her voice penetrate. He tensed, hunching his shoulders slightly – knowing, not what she was going to say, but fearing that it would collapse the careful structure he was trying to build.
- I want you to read some letters I have with me– before the tour of landmarks and architectural sites , before everything is lost.
- Letters? Whose?
- Mine. To you.
- Why do I have to read letters? You're right here.
- She shook her head. Will you read them?
A long pause, while he nursed his suspicions.
- About Maggie?
- Yes and no.
- Okay, I'll read them. He gave up.

Ghosts of Gods and mortals. Not to allow this Paul, this place to bury the past. Mistakes. Missed– takes. His face refused to understand. There was no present – no present worth having without the past. Not to allow it to slip away but to let it invade this moment, filling all the cracks, finally to split apart revealing the nut. The car clambered up a steep endless incline, the sun posing in a southwest display.

- I'll read them but I had hoped we could begin from a different point.
- We can, or we must, mustn't we?
- We're here.

He jumped off the board. The pieces scattered.

Later in the hotel room, after the argument about where Molly was going to stay, a dinner in a typically homey place. After saying goodnight at the door of her room:

- Read them, then call me. Watching him turn away, his jaw set, she called him .
- Paul – don't think there are no Gods here.
He turned and stared at her .
–There weren't until you brought them.

She rested on the bed and closed her eyes. That last grin was a good omen. Perhaps a signal, however unconscious, that he was willing to try to fashion an alembic a hermetic vessel, in which they could struggle to be free. And suddenly the resolve, the strangling purpose that had carried Molly along, through the drive, the insistence on a hotel, the silly dinner, snapped. A lover's meeting far from the grotto of love, an empty bed, a sword between them heralding separate journeys – while somewhere in another landscape they ran perpetually toward each other, not touching. Not touching. Not yet.

- What am I supposed to say about these? Pushing the package of letters across the table.
-Whatever you say.
- I don't write letters, but I did ask you to come here.
-I still don't know why.
- Why I asked, or why you came.
-Both. That was a lie. Part of another time, part of Amerika. She could see herself being stubborn in his eyes.
-Well – we're friends.
-That's a strange way of putting it.

- Anyway – I should have looked up Jean–Claude. I didn't realize - A lot of things.

- No.

-And still don't? Is that what you're saying?

-That's what I'm saying.

-I don't know what you're saying. He flared. People raised their heads to look at us embarrassing him. The world intruded loudly and for the first time I acknowledged the fact that I was not in Greece. Our privileges were different here – not exiles on an island, out of time, out of place.

- Back off, Molly. Give me some room. His ears still red, he whispered furiously.

- All right.

She had a fleeting urge to tip over the table, throw coffee in his face, screech. Thinking of the faces behind her with their disturbed vacations, their images of being laid back and serene scattered so much rotten fruit at their feet. She sighed. Paul looked up.

The rage abates, all the imagined losses conflated with real ones and as it fades she knows with a deep despair that this scene does not truly belong, that it speaks another language altogether, a language which confuses her – attracts and repels; even so, she allows it as she permits herself to know the worst.

Change has occurred. This writing is, at last identified as merely the witness to change – another voice in this book. The witness to change so we have come at last to grasp again is permanently changed.

FOURTEEN

HAVING DECLARED she had in fact had an ordinary life, it became doubtful. Madness, hospitalization, substituted a layer of non–reality for the previous reality – or was it the other way around? Then the scattered Notes, the characters' slippery biographies made her wonder about the source of her instability and confusion. The source of the Nile as Dr. Freud would say.

Meanwhile she has Alex pondering his next move in Rome on the Via Veneto wearing mirrored sunglasses and flicking his tail. The feral intuition rotates the board; he extrapolates on Maggie's death, prepares his counter moves.

Angelica stirs; tries to remember the trail to the monastery that day and most importantly the placement of the people. Particularly Alex. In the taverna when they had finally returned to the village:

"It was an accident" – defensive, angry, final.

"Was it?" Maggie's body lying, a bird fallen out of the sky, a flash of color on the dead, gray rocks below.

"Everybody believes what they want to believe – what was that guide's name? Takis? He came running, shouting, "she jump, she jump".

"Of course he had to say that. What about his tourist business. The church and all – a bad omen.

"Angelica, look, the road was rotten, the donkey slipped, she toppled."

"Maybe."

She doesn't grasp the significance of what she writes, it baffles her. The feeling of a murder lurks somewhere, keeps re-appearing . Something has been killed. Are they all guilty? Did she jump? She feels disgruntled today staring at nothing. The occasional rustle of a movement behind her, like mice she thinks. Isn't it time for a cogent interpretation she wonders and hears laughter.

Part of the rehabilitation program at the hospital included the attending of several sessions of group therapy. One long term in and out patient (there you are a patient, without patience, later in a cozier temenos you graduate to client - a dubious promotion which feels more disconnected– with endless patience) staggering around on an overdose of an anti-psychotic, would unexpectedly appear at my elbow to inform me that the rooms were bugged by the CIA; "don't eat that," he'd mutter, pointing at my dinner, and as he wobbled off – "you know, they gave you the wrong doctor."

He was excluded from the therapy sessions, organized by the ghost of Samuel Beckett. The serious nurse/social worker confronts six drugged disoriented people in various stages of paranoia, depression, anxiety neurosis, with a panoramic array of hallucinations and delusions. "I'd like you to list the attributes of a mentally healthy person – of course nobody is all of those things," she says smugly. In halting voices the learned responses begin to emerge: 1. trust 2. compassionate 3. understanding 4. independent 5. humor 6 patience 7. inner strength 8. self–aware 9. responsible 10. assertive 11. reasonable expectations of self and others 12 loving 13 good self image 14 confidence 15 capable 16 positive attitude 17 well integrated 18 good support system 19 honesty 20 good communications 21 religion 22 happy 23 able to express anger appropriately 24 good coping mechanisms 25 physically healthy 26 intelligence 27 self respect 28 objectivity 29 self control 30 aware of limitations 31 security 32 liking oneself 33 discipline 34 accepting of self and others 35 realization of others needs, own needs and the ability to give and take.

❋

She grasps the knowledge that she doesn't know who has been speaking all along and it comes as a relief. There always is a knowing that is never told in the sessions –the body in travail vomiting up what seem to be pieces of bloody chunks of flesh, of insects trailing cellular memories; commando attacks.

She resists the impulse to batter Analyst. To destroy forever this sacred space. To weep. To find nothing but contempt for weeping. If she permitted weeping she fears the water would end in drowning all of them, would never find a way to the sea. She would find herself on a corner hauling this analysis in a plastic garbage bag.

Nevertheless it all continues denying, defying the death of speaking.

Liquor smells like death, whiskey terrifies the body. There is screaming in the ether of a bar. There on a narrow strip of wood, a tiny girl dances to show off for her father. He lifted her up there. His friends watch her smile, her curls bouncing against the lined up bottles behind the bar. The ether is screaming, warning, trying to stop her. Suddenly there is no sound; she is deaf, blind, gone.

The next frame is the bathroom of the bar – she sees her feet down there, her shoes and socks, someone behind her is holding her arms down, in a whirl of wetness slimy stuff all over her, she can't see their faces.

IS THIS PORNOGRAPHIC
IS THIS PORNOGRAPHIC?

She remembers a coat she was wearing that day. But nothing else she recognized as herself was ever there again.

It should be time for the mother, a mother, she thinks. Is this what is happening here in this tomb/womb where she waits to be – born –terminated? But analysis is interminable, isn't it? There is something here of mother, something of the not–mother she knew/never knew. Metaphors and stories – A man stands at the gate of the mother's door –Here she cannot see Analyst – that is familiar, a known separation.

Is that your mother? NO.

Is that your mother? No. The city is my mother, I found myself here in the city. How did you get here? Metaphysically.

Nothing bursts forth. Each utterance is terrified of a sound. Let's stop this session – let's have a short session today – She's confused. She could leave anyway – not telling, saying words about another appointment, a conflict. She drifts to a time of the madness, a time of Demeter and Persephone in a field. A space of trees, of connection, of beginning.

A reading she wrote one day to explain, grasp.

"Mother, to you I will tell the whole story exactly and frankly." Persephone to Demeter and oh, how the grief of Demeter is music to the ears of the child. How her depression is a vindication, an echo and witness drawing the mother and daughter together. How the daughter waits in the darkness of the underworld while she is searched for, sought but not found, knowing the mother is seeking her, knowing she has not been abandoned. The desolation Demeter produces in her rage, her denial of the Gods of Olympus, her proof of continuing love, all tell Persephone robbed of the daylight world of flowers and friends, that her absence is noted, that she is missed, longed for, grieved for and not forgotten. That her mother has *seen* her, that her face is remembered. For in the darkness she can no longer see herself or remember her name. She has become the Queen of the Underworld. the Queen of the Dead.

FIFTEEN

IN A MALL THERE is a children's clothing store. She, Queen of the Underworld, puts pieces of candy in the pockets of the uninhabited dresses: the dreams of mothers. Hoping to sweeten the fate of the dresses, the bodies in the dresses, the charming dresses.

From here you can say anything; as before said, there is no moon, no sun. These words arise ghostly, unending, spoken from no where they drift across space.

Appropriate to the Underworld – we have to begin the thoughts of death.

Who is Maggie?

She becomes confused during the sessions – to whom is she speaking? Haven't I mentioned the book before? Here –to you behind me rustling the papers of my file (although she knows Analyst writes down the notes later). Maggie is a character in the book, she died without a sound – she was thrown off a mountain, she fell off the donkey, she sacrificed herself in the eruption of the hermetic island. There are too many stories to tell, this room is not large enough, the world is not large enough. Perhaps the Underworld is the only place with enough space. There no death lurks.

At last she finds a fragment of mutual reality.

"He called me last night. He was very upset. What's going on he wants to know, how much money do you think we have, he asks, everyone is worried about you, he says, your daughter misses you". Daughter?

And?

And? She disappears, she doesn't hear him, this urgent noise. And? She has to stay here longer, she whispers at the wire. It's only an hour away and I try to see you as much as I can, she murmurs.

There is that persistent sense of doom coming here to these encounters. It's this other there, waiting and pretending not to wait for a sign, a word. But the word slips away behind the new mask/masque –the analysis mask–u–raid on reality.

Listen, she says, it was better before all this, before the madness, before the analysis, happier...... this discourse peters out, ends in dots, dissolves. A gray hand from the Underworld pulls the words away. This analytic stability, this structured recapitulation – partialized by exclusions, eruptions taking place on islands, or in malls, or in lost bits of written messages from characters –is full of holes, is confining, produces fears.

Long ago I was happy, she thinks. No. Long ago you were depressed often, you screamed in your sleep, you ate mangoes for a year until you could feel your nerves dangling like loose wires out of your arms, you had migraines, you threw up often, you couldn't get out of bed once for three months.

Is that true?

The memory of Crete arrives as solace. Although

the book is continually swallowed by the madness, by the Analysis, Angelica remembers a day.

"'We start out in early morning. The cicadas wildly talking, the crowing of cocks in the far off trees.

Alex is in high spirits. His usually harsh mouth is stretched into a difficult smile. Our sweaters are tied around our waists and flap about our knees.

––You don't like to climb mountains, do you? You think it's foolish, all that effort.

––I say nothing, stumbling behind him frightened by his indifferent back. Of course, it's true that I climb for him, because I want to appear brave, because I want to prove something.

He leaps over peoples gardens trying to avoid the vegetables. I follow gingerly. Do you know where the path is?

––What path, he laughs, we begin at the bottom, right? Well, this is the bottom.

We clamber up, rocks careening down beneath our feet. He looks back occasionally – to see if I have fallen?

To see if I've given up?

I trip and slide, once my ankle is caught between two stones. Then it's noontime. A pine forest, dark and inviting, the ground welcoming my hot body. In the distance the sea in turmoil, blinding mirror of sun, tiny dots of people on the beach, an unfinished painting, houses clinging to the steep rocky hills, lichen, a fantastic sea flora. I look down the mountain side and a scent of freedom rises up to greet me."

The ceiling stares down at her, so she shuts her eyes against its demands. So, she thinks, there in the constant dissolution of the Underworld there is no fear of change – here the clinging to an unidentified object begins, and necessarily in its wake the terror of dissolution. What can be said about that? The picture has developed as a negative. What can be said about that?

In the early morning she wakes to the sound of the sea, dislocated, and sees the old woman again.

the old woman standing on the shore
behind her keeping watch   the others starting
a small fire   she turns and the tears streaking
her cheeks fall unattended   her skirts are touched
by the wet sand   they look up as she approaches
what torrid times   the heat rises   from our
bodies and leaves signs   in the air of our passing
the sweat mirrors the sea   this is the time
for salt   this is the time for   dryness with
only the sound of insects   the red eats the black
the   black devours the red   nothing can
grow here   this is the fasting place   the place of
burning the place of waiting in the sun   now the
sea   can   only be a sight a sound   the
sand must be our bed   their stricken faces are
covered with seawater   their hands are folded in
their laps

SIXTEEN

AFTER VISHNU HAD burnt the universe to ashes at doomsday and then flooded it with water, he slept in the midst of the cosmic ocean.

Now, if we closely examine the contents of the madness we find that there is a certain similarity to the famous case of Schreber the German judge who went mad as a result of torture in his early childhood. The case is described as soul murder.

THESE THINGS DON'T HAPPEN

IT'S ALL BECAUSE OUR SOCIETY IS TOO PERMISSIVE

IT'S ALL BECAUSE OUR SOCIETY IS NOT PERMISSIVE ENOUGH

She sees a different way to read a text on Vishnu:
One day she slipped out of the God's mouth and saw the world and the ocean shrouded in darkness. She did not recognize herself there, because of God's illusion, and she became terrified. Am I crazy or dreaming? I must be imagining that the world has disappeared, for such a calamity could never really happen. Then she was swallowed again and as soon

as she was back in the belly of the god, she thought the vision had been a dream.

There were wild flowers in the field the day the madness began. She picked a few to put in her coffin.

Maggie's coffin.

Angelica refuses to believe that Maggie is gone.

Sometimes she blames Alex, sometimes it's Paul. Then it was a sacrifice, then it was an accident, she remains persistently confused..

Maggie would never agree to analysis anyway.

Would not bother to collect all the yellow lined, white, small and large pieces of paper. To write them down again. To encode them, to decipher them.

Maggie has no loyalty to process, to time, to grasping reality. Angelica finds segments of Maggie's body as she unpacks her boxes in a New York sublet.

"And finally nothing but a sea gull circling close to a shattered sea, distant mountains in a mauve haze. Meridian of love, cataclysm of desire. We must expect the worst – not death but life."

There is a confusion here, a gap, an uncertainty about which is which, a poem by Neruda that Maggie liked.

"A lo sonoro llega la muerte, como un zapato sin pie, como un traje sin hombre, llega a golnear con un anillo sin piedras y sin dedo, llega a gritar sin boca, sin lengua, sin garganta."

And it is so apt. trying to speak from Maggie's place of death with "no mouth, no tongue, no throat."

She wakes up with a terrible earache, desperate because by now the body speak is recognizable. Nevertheless she puts oil in the ear, keeps it warm, carries it to the pale ivory room with leather chairs which only the Analyst sits in. The patient client, a fish on dry land, gasps on the dry couch. She knows the earache is important, she knows and lets it escape awareness, begins with the difficulties of writing, of the nausea that arrives in the wake of words. In the ensuing silence the ear speaks to the waiting ear of the Analyst in language which Analyst imagines is comprehensible.

First there was the void for two years, then at seven she appeared with a mastoid: there was a friendly doctor at the bedside, there was sulphur, there were books and paper dolls, and manikins to dress, there were children without faces or names to help with homework, there was three months. And two men.

Friends of the aunt ?

Larry and Bob. Larry had red hair and freckles. Bob was dark with pale skin. Larry was skinny, Bob was chunky.

They played games with her?

They came to visit the sick little girl?

DID ANYONE SEE THEM?

There is a child floating in the room high above the sprawled white body under Larry. The bodies' nerves are howling with the wolves in the tundra the bodies' limbs are obedient to the sounds from his mouth the hands close around the child's neck to close off all possibility of speech forever all memory of language.

This child is deaf and mute.

Death is her friend.

She recounts memory in a flat voice to the ear of the other and later remarks the rash encircling her neck.

She arrives in a turtleneck sweater for the next session.

SEVENTEEN

SHE READ SOMEWHERE that the position from which women speak may be, like the voice of the mother she first heard, outside time, plural, fluid, bisexual, and decentered.

Nevertheless this speech eludes any articulation and in the sessions she still stumbles mutely through a language teeming with demons, traps which open to plunge her into the caverns of non–sense.

Oh, like Marguerita's death?

How can it remain irretrievable, when she can re–write it. Merely words on paper? Another fairy tale collapsed in on itself, turning ever back to the beginning, unable to reach a resolution. The little girls are disinherited. The goose girl still speaks to the severed head of a horse. The King/Magician pursues the hero, hides himself with the powerful magic of blood and fear. And Maggie drifts down to the sea, a blown leaf, at the bottom carried off by a dark man, her arm gliding on the sea air..

Well, let's suppose this is doing something, she is saying, but not at all what was expected. She hears the question clearly, although only the leather on the chair behind her made a sound. Oh, to be resolved, bandaged into place, glued together, training in acceptance of limits, of damage beyond repair, to resume, assume a survival.

Instead of this non–geometry, this consistent fragmentation, this stranger body never the same two days at a time, this lapse, this gap, this return, circling without circumference.

How could it be otherwise when the patient is not there, here in fact, to administer to? What is brought is addressed it seems, in this "talking cure" – cure for talking out of turn?

A thought intrudes – the book contains the analysis, not the other way around.

Just as the two exiled princesses surround, encapsulate the King/Magician, just as the goose girl, in the field with the sheep, singing her chants to blow the goose boy's hat away, is beyond the confines of the castle. Waiting, yes. More than waiting too. And the princesses?

> After they arrived on the island of safety, nurtured by the gentle spirits, they grew marvelously, as different as night and day. One was dark, the other fair, one was bold the other reflective, one was sturdy, the other delicate. In spite of that their love was the chain that bound them together with tenderness. When they were fifteen the spirits held counsel. Although they knew that the murderous king lived, they also knew that the world was large; that to keep the children on the island would deprive them of their destiny, their fortune. So with great hope and great fear for their safety, they agreed to send them off with many instructions to guide them; with tokens of magic to protect them; with warnings of places too dangerous to explore.

They set sail on the great ocean with sadness and joy in their hearts for they knew that nothing would ever be as lovely as the island, as filled with magic, as bright with color. But they also knew that if they stayed, one day, they would see the life they might have had and it would fill them with terrible sorrow. The life that was meant for them, the fortune that was theirs by birthright which had been stolen. For many years they wandered the chiaroscuro of the world. They underwent many adventures, which are recounted in another story than this. Until one day they heard of the young man banished to the ends of the earth and of the evil perpetrated upon him by the wicked King. The young man had become famous in the land as many prayed to him when their cause seemed hopeless and were helped. The bold dark lady wished to aid him, to seek him out, to go to the ends of the earth. Her sister had become a seer, giving succor to many and, being more frail, did not wish to make such an arduous journey. So, amid tears of farewell, with abundant good wishes and promises of perpetual help, they parted.

Analyst has installed several young trees she notices at the next session. She remarks too that the familiar blanket, the couch, the chairs, the ceiling form a space she might move in very slowly. Even the squeaks of leather, the small noises of dress material on nylon are comforting.

She is not so alarmed at the smallness of this patient she has become. The book is not the patient. Not even the client. That is a comfort too.

He called again last night in a better mood – less strident, we could even talk about a visit, after all it's only an hour away. Talking to Daisy is hard on the phone, she is only four. The guilt is overwhelming – leaving her like that–although she likes his mother very much. Will this leave indelible scars on her? Will she be lying on a couch like this someday too?

Angelica persists in writing to Alex, piling up letter after letter:

"You always wanted to divide Marguerita and me into two, to polarize us. You knew you could manipulate me using charm – not her at all. She escaped you, in fact she escaped everyone else as well. Your hope was that I didn't know that, was not included in her strategies. I suppose you were saving me for later – being too cowardly to ever really be with her – at least back in the real world. Somewhere moving from your past to your future there dwelt the image of a normal life – you understand what I mean –a picture, a stone frieze. Well, she and I are one – now more than ever; ultimately. Try to understand it as best you can. When or if you are able to see both of us – it won't seem so strange.

I know now that you did not push her really – but a nagging doubt still remains – perhaps only your presence contributed – should I hold you to blame for that?"

There have been no dreams for a long time.

Only a quick fall into rocklike sleep. Or sometimes an alert wakefulness punctuated by fitful reading, restless heat beating at the doors of her skin.

EIGHTEEN

THE SYMPTOMS CARRY her back into death, to spaces without walls, voids of no–sound containing moving images: the hell of desire in disembodied parts. She has read that lost objects can never be re-found only substituted for. Here no language exists, no likeness is possible, metaphor dies of incomprehension.

Only an eye is present, a cyclopean focus. The struggles of the body in terror –the nervous system raging, failing –happen to no–one, no person punctuated by the eerie wailing of neurons, ganglions shutting down, closing the doors to an inferno.

Analyst cannot know this, she thinks afterward, no– one can know this because she cannot know it. But the eye sees and makes words appear on a slate. There were other children, the white gaze of a light, the body tumbling in an abyss of hands and other parts, women with lipstick and dogs.

Why does this Cyclops insist on seeing this?

Analyst is innocent behind the couch expecting the shape of a narrative. But translation is impossible. These events defy telling. There is nothing to tell of them, no residue, no fissure to allow a symbol to form, a recognizable shape. This event stands, a dolmen, smooth, with no referents in the world to grasp its sense.

The Cyclops saw everything, and the eye could not blink, but an Angel of Mercy arrived to gently close the lid in sleep, to pour sweet balm into the ravaged body, to affix the seal on the door, a whirling wheel to guard. Until. This moment.

NINETEEN

WENT TO DINNER last night, she is saying, and forgot all about this room. She mustn't tell Analyst that this therapy is too narrow a space; that in Zen parlance the eyes are fixed but look at what has happened to the mouth.

The book is trapped in the mystery of its resolution; in a seesaw of eternal return to that one instant of Maggie's silent plunge. Jean-Claude is a ripped up letter to Maggie found on the island by Angelica .

"Dear M

I thought I saw you yesterday. I followed her down the street, drinking in her walk, your walk, but then just as suddenly the illusion broke and I realized that it had been my hunger for you that had produced a doppelganger. How can you be duplicated? I write into your silence not knowing what it may mean. Not understanding what happened. Others tell me that it is good that my perplexity has become mute and simply lives inside me a petrified tree. Where are you now?"

He had a friend, an enormous friend, who stayed at the villa a while. For some reason connected with a childhood drama he was called Poo Bah. He would spend hours in the kitchen after shopping all morning and concoct feasts. And he too had his story of death and betrayal. He used to quote Cyril Connolly saying that inside every fat man there is a thin one trying to get out. Jean-Claude's sister saw him in New York, and writes that Poo Bah is going down like a great battleship with a small hole, at a leisurely pace, one more bottle a week.

These men struggling to surface in the book, in spite of their New York biographies, in the face of numerous name changes, barely emerge. Alex seems far too basically narcissistic and one sided, and his transformation into Paul is not a vast improvement. Jean-Claude is a phantom, Poo Bah was consumed in the fire of madness and analysis.

She puts all the papers in a cardboard box.

Blocked. Is this more resistance? "It is a fatal flaw of the ego psychologists to look on defense as resistance, as something to be 'worked through'. Rather, it too is to be permitted to speak".

Not yet. The words, syllables, letters, descend. The Queen of the Underworld can hear them, as she sips wine at dinner. The food goes down with the words. Later the headache hammers the words into powder, a potion which produces nausea. The toilet bowl waits to receive the offerings. Hysteria imagines bringing this to Analyst, these outpourings.

The world is still there after all, she thinks, with its newspapers and self-help books, its descriptions and explanations. She must be there too because danger signals at the next session.

Is too much going out or is too much coming in? Danger in the heaviness, terror in the lightness. The balance has been shattered; homeostasis an impossible nightmare, a battle in blindness, with no moon.

The others say beware of bulimia. Anorexia..
Anorexia or death or worse than death.

A text says:

...(seed) is generated inside the body of a man and
...(the seed of a woman) is generated in the body of
a woman after the intake of food.

Carrion. She was fed on death; uninhabited flesh
puffed up with hatred, swollen with rage, weapons of
power.

Even so, she despises crying on the couch
suspended in Analyst's sacred space. She turns her
head toward the wall, pulling up the blanket, blocking
out the scratching pen signaling Analyst's presence.
Negating the room shutting down, cutting off, blocking,
blocking.

Until a vision comes of the old woman on the beach
with her feet in the ocean, her toes grasping the sand,
her skirts hiked up around her waist. This old woman
is staring, is waiting. Far up the shore the others are
unmoving in front of the guttering fire. They don't
watch her as she lifts her arms, and her mouth opens
to eject a cascade of seeds turned into small pebbles,
a shrouded movement cast into the foaming sea.

TWENTY

THE ANGLE OF VISION, from this position, is too flat, she thinks. Analysis doesn't take into account the curvature of the earth, the rotation of the planet.

You know, she is saying, that flies see multiple images? The problem is you are trying to reconstruct a past which has no existence as continuity – it's all about the angle of vision.

The book poses a similar dilemma. Angelica sees the landscape rising out of foam on a rotating field–the waves disintegrating the shoreline - the remainder, detritus.

Then on the other side of islands, of analysis, of urgent phone messages penetrating in their desire to have done with re-collecting – is the ineluctable truth, inescapable and without sense –of madness and the past fragmenting in the body. In fact, there is no body here except a cellular transparency, a time capsule.

So, she thinks sourly, again supine, once more an articulation –what is Analyst fashioning of this collection?

Now there is an image of a woman in a mall, she forgets her name in the record shop, but signs the credit slip anyway with another name – the clerk doesn't notice she is not there. He imagines her a real person. She, on the other hand, is unknowingly re-enacting a snippet of a drama, a twisted piece of the past, squeezed through a distorted lens. She has purchased a record entitled "That's No Way to Treat a Lady". She deposits it on a table belonging to a coffee shop two doors away and waits, nervously, to see who will offend, who is the offender, who will pick it up. Because the film has been cut in so many places – a scene appears without antecedents, without denouement. Detritus.

It is a case of a rage burned into ashes and blown away on the wind.

This rotation reveals a blank filled with sadness for something that is no longer remembered. Even grief evaporates, although her cheeks are wet – why?

However, now that the autobiography has failed, cannot be maintained, peels away, she senses the absence as a presence – a presence pregnant with longing, a wraith consuming all substance.

The earth is kind, it carries along graveyards without markers, until they pass from view, vanish from the gaze of the living, consigned to the gentle care of the Queen of the Underworld. When the planet shifts, plows under these ashen voids, she too shivers, perplexed by their arctic movements, trembles under their sightless gaze.

Fractured, she tells a dream of herself as a manikin being examined by a group of shadowy men – her flesh is ice – there are no nipples on her breasts, no vagina – smooth without openings, and the horror of a painted face. The men keep looking, continue to probe until she wakes up, struggles into clothes; manages a cup of coffee and burns her throat awake.

Perhaps, she wonders, Dr. Feingold was right after

all, and the world is flat. This treatment takes place behind a scrim, faltering, Analyst a shadow puppet, ready to collapse, forcing a readjustment, another shift. The description of this view expires under the pressure of language, becomes a liquid, an acid eating holes in therapy, in Analyst's chair; threatening to dissolve the couch itself.

TWENTY-ONE

YOU KNOW, SHE SAYS my mind treasures a Van Gogh – Garden of the Poets – there was a smell of flowers in that corner of the museum And a Cezanne – houses with trees reflected in the water. It takes a long time before the eye can tell where the water begins, where the bank ends and the sky is not there – is merely white canvas, as if the whole were suspended in the space of the retina. And then, along side these images there is Joyce with his golden Irish voice holding a wake for the world – the puny world.

There have been burnings of old photographs; of this face smiling at the camera daring to pretend to humanity. Hands holding a baby, the baby reaching out toward the invisible face behind the camera – a lens though which she sees that other face grinning in smugness, sly with its power, content with its terror. Burnings of these photographs since there is a time for the photograph album.

You know, she says again, when he died I smelled rotting meat and ate no food for days – food for maggots, maggots as food.

They say rage is red, but rage is an ebony pillar sunk into the earth, eluding the sky, a white sky. When it cracks the redyellowblue flames greedily engulf the Van Goghs, the Da Vincis, the Cezannes, the pages of books – all eaten to gray powder.

He is chased through the stratosphere, relentlessly pursued – caught – he is dismembered.

The Furies arrive and seeing the pillar, seeing the ashes, flee – sealing the gates forever.

That place, that site/sight is flooded – the waters above, the waters below converge. Silt is traced by the movement of waves. They say no person can ever find a story there. In a million years the fish will glide in blue refracted light.

That being the case she rescinds all permission for Analyst to create slides.

Or a presentation.

Whose analysis is this? she muses, and it's too small anyway. However, still effective on a band, in a pinch, in a car on the highway.

TWENTY-TWO

WHAT WAS DREADED has occurred – as predicted by gypsy women on a beach in Greece – all the stories have evaporated, have died, like Maggie so quietly–. This is a slide show – only a humming of the projector – no narrator, no narration.

> slide into a bathroom
> slide of red water in the toilet bowl
> slide of a scissors
>> of a kitty–foot falling
>> an ear tip an ear tip
>> a kitty foot falling
>> a tail hanging in the air
> slide onto the face of a little girl without eyes or mouth or ears
>> a blank slide
>> the machine stops humming

A woman without legs, a woman whose legs won't work, a woman crawls out of the bathroom, struggles to the bed, falls, cascades, dissolves into sleep.

Analyst cannot present a slide show, she has no permission. This is a demonstration but
A SLIDE SHOW CANNOT BE PRESENTED.

TWENTY-THREE

LET'S TALK ABOUT PROTECTION. The Protection Racket.

The protection noise. Maggie's death fits here shrouded in the slippage off the cliff, the lack of noise. Although the book is effaced at this moment, here in this dyadic space, packed in cartons somewhere else, this shadow of Maggie is present in absence.

According to the Laws of Manu: whosoever has committed incest with his mother must tear off his genitals and, carrying them in his hand, will go towards the West. Towards death, towards extinction.

But another case: whosoever has violated, tortured, dismembered his daughter must?

Must......

Faltering on a cliff the daughter seeks protection, yes, and what of the punishment?

And what is the crime?

Is it incest? Where is it written?

The first door of the maze, the labyrinth opens, in fact is a vortex, a tornado sucking the girl in head first. Back into the mouth of the mother seeking safety, becoming the mother in a landscape of women, being the mother to achieve the punishment of the father.

The second door appears, is closed, even barred, sealed with confusion, with misunderstanding, with wild hope unwilling to be deferred.

Ah.... it is not meant to be this punishment so dearly wished, so counted on, dreamed and seen a thousand times. For the eyes of Oedipus are plucked in plague around the mother and he the son. Here there is only a triad – Mother, Father, Son. The tornado with a deluded intensity brings a failure, a major missed–take – a double take. The maze shifts again in despair; follow the thread black or red there is no exit.

This is too sad, she thinks, shifting on the couch. This is a bad joke, this helping/healing/curing/ drying up/ a piece of beef jerky. Is this where it ends then, terminates rather? This existential no–exit? Is Analyst working through the resistance to find a coded agony of furious helplessness, of eternal victimization without recourse? Even she, clamped to the couch, contorted into a mythological shape of miserable discontinuous attachment, a monster never named, or named unrecognizable, can see through closed eyes the triad which refuses to budge.

It is clear enough now, even lucid, the mirage of punishment, an oasis with filthy water, an oasis forever receding in a desert of women transforming into mothers and daughters to find redress.

The Law is clear, even lucid. The Father can the mother, the Son must not the mother.

The Father must not.....

The Father must not......

The law is unclear, muddy with the blood of daughters seeping into the earth, polluting the ocean.

The Queen of the Underworld, released from Hell, wandering in a Mall, risen from the death of desire, of loving which in the Middle Ages was a grave a really terrible disaster.

She is disgruntled because the secret text written away from this place has crept in, has found a hole in the narrative woven for the edification of Analyst. And then:

In this center of nothing coherent she sees a disturbing truth or perhaps another lie, another door in this curving space, this DNA molecule, spiraling back on itself – for she knows she read that before at the very beginning, on the first page, written down without knowledge, read in confusion. As a sign, a cipher of murder.

And that circling up and down shows a picture of herself, of all things, protecting Analyst.

Protecting this effigy of a session, blinding this Other so she will not have to know. She and she too. Even she whose Cyclopean eye saw all the story.

But why?

Not yet, please not yet. She sees in a spontaneous image on the infernal couch, the boxes opening in her room, the boxes of Maggie, of Angelica of Alex/Paul, of Jean-Claude of Greece and more. The telephone ringing, and her daughter's voice stumbling, but firm, perplexed and confident.

She sees this daughter's face, and gradually a body comes into focus bringing an odor of Van Gogh's roses. Of never imagined sweetness. At last, she spends the rest of the session weeping real tears, wiping her eyes and blowing her nose. She even gets a drink of water in the bathroom before she leaves. Outside again, the light mingles with her hair, brushes up to her sweater, slides down her leg. That, however, is much too much to notice:

She recalls the phrase that was an explanation at the beginning of the book, something about love, about being awakened to love "a grave and really terrible disaster, not only for herself, for whom torture and fire were in prospect, but also for her lover", for her lover or she thinks now grasping the slide show, for anything she might love.

Without warning she thinks; it might be possible at some time to provide permission for the presentation of the slide show.

TWENTY-FOUR

WITH THIS NEW ERUPTION onto the scene of the analysis, this awful perturbation, a palpitation of the heart, a hopeless nausea supervenes.

At first it was roses, the smell of the daughter, but now it is the danger of roses, the dangers of redness or is it blackness she means.

Before, at the beginning of this interminable process she froze and trembled in darkness before a Stone; now it seems it is the light, the sunlight that touched her, which freezes her bones, congeals her blood. This Analyst has now become a target, a threat. Is she too perfect, this face in a chair somewhere or is it that the Analyst constantly, overwhelmingly fails, falls into a black hole dragging the patient along?

She is furious to imagine that in fact what was hidden, covered, cowered in the Underworld has been exposed, revealed, touched on, changed, changing.

What refuses to acknowledge any difference here still insists on a silence, on a perfection of muteness. In spite of last time(s), there will be no further story. The narrative will come to a halt, she thinks. Right now.

All well and good, however the session continues anyway. Something will speak, it will seep in through the cracks, destroying, eroding, effacing her intentions.

Well then, no nausea will have worked, no headache will intervene in this historical reality – this anti–autobiography. And what is that history?

That the daughter died and went to hell, first in a bar. That she was resurrected and died again in the bathroom, flushed down the toilet with a tiny tiger colored kitty in red toilet water into the dark pipes of the Underworld; that she came back again, a wraith waiting, wanting and was finally strangled at seven years old in her bedroom, abandoned there by her mother.

Then she was Queen of the Underworld.

When she was alive, did she fool the mother? Did the mother want to be fooled? The protection racket is too loud. In the event, the event of having no mother can there be a daughter?

It's like this Analyst – is she fooled? or does she prefer to imagine process in lieu of realities? Does she know or not know? She is supposed to be the one– supposed to know the story, the resolution, to piece together the narrative. But this patient client thinks the Analyst believes she is crafty– this is only half the puzzle – only a turn in the maze to throw her off the scent. The chair creaks with scribbling on a pad. Sometimes the Analyst speaks, recites an interpretation, muses on reality.

She actually muses aloud: You know, she is saying, Freud discusses an amnesia that starts with the concept of total recall as the objective of the analysis but ends up with a discussion of fantasy. So we have Freud seeming to endorse a concept which was most completely to undermine the idea of the cure as the retrieval of a real occurrence.

So ha, the patient thinks. She cannot fathom these truths. Now she's talking about Freud to squirm away from reality. But how could she fathom these revelations when the patient cannot either??

So in reality there is Persephone trapped in Hades and Demeter sleeps in ignorance.. No escape, she thinks, except in the mad afternoon in the country house, a memory of a real occurrence, an at least partially witnessed event. And the secret event, her rising out of a grave place, the place of the impending pipes to the country house. Does the Analyst remember this piece of mostly verifiable concrete reality?

Did she tell the Analyst this at the commencement of these encounters. Yes.

She arises like Spring and Demeter is all around, in the very air she breathes, touching her with sunlight which cannot hurt her eyes or freeze her bones. No. Instead, in this real occurrence of madness at Eleusis, Persephone, neurasthenic, anorexic no longer, races, flies joyous in the arms of love to a river in which the mystery of transformation occurs; in a moment, a single moment when the water meets her skin, she is Artemis.

The protector, the avenger the perfect daughter with a dead mother. The eternal daughter, virgin, with her arrows aimed, sly and sharp.

All right, interpret that occurrence, she gloats.

Now both are present/absent – speaking/silent. There truly is not a cause for gloating, she thinks, not with this hammering in the solar plexus, this imminent nausea, perhaps tonight a migraine.

Polarization in ambiguity.

This dyad is collapsing confronted by the transference.

Now what?

TWENTY-FIVE

DOES ANY OF THIS have to do with psychology, she thinks once more, always it appears on the couch. Or even psychoanalysis. As to dreams, the material, the alchemical lead of this experience, they arrive piecemeal, dismembered. A girl of five grown six feet tall, sucking her thumb; a dim picture of someone she once knew, pregnant; a sense of madness, of dissolution; of paranoia.

Misapprehensions. Mistaken identities. This Analyst for example, perhaps she is about to pounce, her fangs bared. A likely story is that Analyst is producing a tangle of interpretation, is directing the patient into this confusion for a reason, a psychoanalytic reason. It seems there must be a significance in the fact that the patient is falling apart, that the client's body is manifesting symptoms which were never there before this talking cure, or talking torture, began.

Consider the book. Angelica has faded, the narrator has vanished into the blind alleys of New York somewhere in Amerika; not to be found. Jean–Claude, entombed on a spiritual quest, unreachable while Alex has divided himself into two, himself and a Paul, a queer mitosis – severed from himself –half swinging his legs in Rome cafes, ogling women, avoiding contact, ignoring the past dogging his heels. He must believe that success lies in foregoing entrapment, escaping all lures in the imagination of movement. His other half, Paul, is condemned to diligence without hope of rescue. Only Maggie haunts this scene of language in travail, of explosive utterance; of the body of the patient in labor. Her mysteries captivate the gaze; an obsession. An ambivalence. Alive in death, dead to life. Switching and shifting, Maggie is a knot, a way of compelling the book to go on, to move while in stasis.

Although fractured, she imagines that the now de–fanged Analyst, the certainly not–neutral Analyst, can offer a statement regarding, pertaining to her condition. She is enormously sophisticated, she fantasies, knowledgeable about this process and/or projecting into the charged space between them a salient remark.

When the traumatic elements – grounded in an image which has never been integrated –draw near holes, points of fracture appear in the history? That must be the statement.

She is drawn, even when alone, although resisting, to Maggie, Marguerita (a flower that Persephone saw) and thence to the fading voice of Angelica at war, Angelica writing the account of a fractured image. Of a hope which will not die.

"Marguerita is not dead. I don't mean sentimentally or psychologically – I mean she never fell off the cliff that day. The donkey did. She hid behind the rocks, she watched us fevered, frantic. She felt our relief. Too premature it was, for either way, dead or alive, there is no termination, no victory. Indeed, our satisfaction with that presumed finality was laden with its own grief. She saw too clearly – some of the time – perhaps she was a bit mad, this Maggie bereft of loyalties, an emotional mercenary.

Maggie, she is saying speaking about the characters as old friends, is capable of speaking the unutterable word of love, despite the curse of the medievalists, yet isn't it so that the "grave and terrible disaster "was visited upon her? But what sacrifices did she make, and what an offering she became. And in the madness this fragment did not appear, was edited out of mind.

Is the Analyst alert to the fact that after Artemis comes hysteria? The threshold of chaos heralded by a sweaty awakening in mid–winter; the unwelcome appearance of the ratty old lady.

> her pipe is gone   she wears a long black cloak
> lined in red fur   her face shadowed in the hood
> the fire is the only light in a moonless night   watch
> me leave this time   alone   while you all tend the
> fire   this is the moment for the forest   the dark
> forest of love captured by the beast the beast
> that sings songs which twist the heart   melodies
> that whither the leaves on the trees rhythms
> pounding   through the earth
> sterilizing the wombs of the animals   this is the
> time to enter the chaos   the glamour of corpses
> the   enchantment of
> reversals

The temenos holds, more or less, in spite of slippage, or refractions and she is saying coldly – he used to sing a horrible song, driving the body into primordial spaces. A song that was a signal for the picture to reverse.

"You always hurt the one you love, the one you shouldn't hurt at all..."

TWENTY-SIX

LET A DREAM SPEAK now, although out of its chronology. Inside this dream undergone in the aftermath, the wake of the hospital encounters, the subject of the dream is traveling down a high mountain pass beside a sleek black horse. Suddenly bandits appear brandishing long knives. The subject of the dream vanishes and the bandits attack the horse, they attempt to slit its throat, they do/don't penetrate the flesh of the horses' neck. The horse furiously is brought to its front knees, unwilling, resisting, the head swiveling in rage, the yellow eyes defiant. The horse screams. This dream is unbearable in its horror. She awakes trembling with the terror and rage, the defiance and the pity.

Inevitably it all fits, since now the goose girl and Falada, the talking horse head, the bodiless/headless horse meet once more. Speech then is at stake. Language the issue: and mother

It's all fading away; the residue is only physiological panic, palpitations, suffocations, a chest collapsed. A blind alley.

Enough of that, she is saying, last weekend the whole family met, mother–in–law, mother, father–in–

law, brother–in–law, daughter, husband. There's no disagreement – everyone agrees it was awful, everyone agrees that it's over now, everyone agrees even more that this treatment is going on too long. She can see herself striving to reach them through glass, across a chasm. The desire to be on their side after all, to be held in ignorant banality, to never have known any of it , precipitated an absence, a lack. When she was able to see again all of them, the others, had shriveled up and blown away leaving her alone, behind the glass. Desire is lethal.

Writing Maggie instructed her in the path to circumvent the love–rays.

At the moment Maggie appeared to Angelica, possibility arrived. Not the time yet for the dark wood, instead Maggie produces a magic lantern show, fireworks on a starless night. She moves stealthily but with abandon; accused of being elusive, discovering a tightrope, she dances in the realm of never wanting, never having, lacking no–thing, all things are possessed.

Try not to get confused – it's not spiritual at all, it's magic survival. It cannot last.

Brash writing. Constructing words to banish Maggie – the paradox of her existence. Just the same, on the other hand, she falls off the mountain, the tightrope, metaphorically?

This analysis, Analyst up against Maggie, must eventually respond, enter the dialogue with her. Grasp the pattern of Maggie – a-causal though she is.

You see, can't you, that Maggie is all about severance and language as a cipher for what is still imprisoned in the dark wood where the old lady is wandering in her black and red cloak.

As a brief addenda to this beginning of the exhumation of Maggie: Angelica imagines Heloise while Heloise dreams of Abelard; and while Maggie, of course, burns in the ice of love, until the Greek sun bakes the mountain.

Anyway, she is saying, being with the family was more difficult than ever. It wasn't smooth, traversing old ruins coupled with lying here roughed up the landscape, opened fissures, created chasms. The contemplation of any more loss is out of the question, she thinks, remembering the family receding; the white trail of an airplane.

TWENTY-SEVEN

INSOFAR AS SHE, at least partially, infects the Analyst with the family, with all the others, with herself, she protects, evades and the text of the book hangs suspended.

Without that ballast, she predicts madness on one side and insanity on the other. A nervous system turned inside out, reversed, traversed in bondage awaits recognition, lurks in dark corners unless the perfect acceptance of the other slavery, the endless dance of family is enjoined.

A discourse on the Count of Monte Cristo, and the subject of non-violent revenge wildly directed at the now familiar visage of Analyst seems too expensive, too blank as well, despite the fact that now Analyst often presents a face of sorts. And because she fully grasps the futility.

Nevertheless, on that discourse hinges a closed opening. Oh, she is able to say the words, while the family dinner proceeds, words swallowed with their meanings, bereft of sense and here too lying down, a willing subject at this point – willing to confess and obtain absolution. To relinquish all desire – to terminate all the narratives, to suddenly walk away. A polished autobiography.

The notion of confession carries an old recurring dream, a ghostly nightmare which haunted adolescence. A building is on fire, perhaps a school building. All the children try to escape; with Grandma's help they run out of the building to find themselves in a menacing wood. A young girl and the Grandma race away from the fire which has attacked the trees behind them. As she turns back to look, out of the flames, untouched by the flames appear three loping lions, nine feet tall, arranged in a pyramid shape. Oh Grandma, they are coming – the fire and the lions. The two come to a crevasse, huge, slicing the wood in half – on this side flames and lions on the other a smooth green sward, rolling hills and a blue sky. At the bottom of the crevasse are hot coals, black and red, red and black. You must confess or else, if you try to leap the chasm you will fall. If you confess you will be carried over to the other side. Grandma says, confess. Yes, yes, but it is forgotten this confession. Confess – or the flaming lions will arrive. It is forgotten. She would awake as no–one, as someone without a name, in mortal terror, eyes wide, hands clutched.

Is this the time of recollection? The ratty old lady, hidden in her cloak of black and red, stalks the woods, she knows that much. It is so quiet there without the howling of the wolves, the chattering of birds. There are places where the fire has eaten the trees, devoured even the earth –once more ocher and black.

There was a sculpture, created in the madness, of a red plastic cup set on fire in the sink, containing pennies, containing burnt out matches plus other objects, objects belonging to other people there. Finally it was a red and black mass, a modern shapeless form thrown out while she was in the hospital. Cast out while the friends whitewashed the house.

Surely Analyst has a comment to make, an insertion, an intrusion. Maybe not.

In that case, she can free associate masking speech, clothing the words in language, setting them out, arranging them to be written.

Red is for roses, for desire, for passion. Red is for rage, black is for death, for darkness for rage for hate for revenge; red is for revenge for hate, black is for love that murders red is for love that murders. See – she can confess it, even so, the desire exists to kill in an arctic place a white place of mirrors. Forever.

TWENTY-EIGHT

IT ALWAYS CHANGES. August arrives with its heated pavements and ritual offerings of fruit, succulent reminders of Spring in the midst of the sense of a parched fading into Autumn. Analysis drifts away on vacation for three weeks. Threads of family extend to cabins in the woods or silhouettes on the beach. Back in the house, wandering the rooms emptied of crazed fears or magic moments, the mirrors blackened, she moves without feet, like an Aborigine through dreamtime.

It's always changing. There is a movement, a rustling under the earth, a sound of spinning, of shuttles whispering. Of a time in which letters from Maggie are read aloud, are written again since she knows the hidden words. She travels in the dreamtime; not fearlessly, in the conceit that she and Angelica can meet. Mocking, even subverting the struggle to write the book, to fix the characters, admitting to the confusion of tongues. A Babel of Notes.

"Angie – the monumental task is to distinguish shadows, while desire strives for a dreamless landscape. To love the moon, the night, to study different degrees of darkness, that is a work. So the thought that the past is over, that life moves on ever more brilliantly illuminated; that events recede, stations scattered and disappearing through the window of a train: all that is vain."

She is not above considering that the profound treasures extracted, mined in the sessions, have been abandoned at the site, given over to the icon of Analyst's knowledge. Relinquished in exchange for absolution, that is Lethe, the waters of forgetfulness. Not difficult to contemplate this barter – when these words, these letters, these parts of bodies, these inscriptions on flesh, not consigned, a/signed burn, grow incandescent, sear and contain the seeds, the burning coals of desire.

"Dear Maggie –

Who could ever fall into your love? A fearsome place without desire, with no reflections, like sailing into the sea where Jean–Claude must become a sailor and is still lost. Where Alex refuses, stands on the shore willing himself deaf to the pure songs making his body tremble. And I, I become Heloise forever wedded to the image of Abelard, vanished in love, fascinated in the absence of my image, enchanted by what you see, that I cannot."

And so, the history repeats itself, the compulsion insists that even there, in the dried bones of Medieval France, in a lesson on the vagaries of epistolary fictions as fact, realities transformed into fictions, she finds the traces of the banishment of desire. Since Heloise is now eternally fading from view as writer, as lover, as nun, erased in the fiction of the creation of "Heloise and Abelard", she, walking in the primordial landscape liberated by August rituals, can see the shaping of her own disappearance.

"Dear Angie – what a furiously alive conceit this imagining of yourself as Heloise to Alex's Abelard. Failing that as Heloise clothed in the singularly uncomfortable habit of a forced servitude, fixated on the last glimpse of the ivory of her body, roughly awakened, yet absent from itself. Left to search there, where last she saw it, at the moment it evaporated, her gaze trapped, like a Unicorn.

Love, Maggie."

TWENTY-NINE

WITHOUT THE BALLAST of weekly exposures, hourly deceits and misapprehensions, she ascends, descends, floats, is enraged or depressed, forgetful in an hallucination of freedom absent from joy, isolated from knowing.

The house is stifling, even in the cool of the evenings echoing the sounds of street life. She is suspended in this limbo of non–realization, a rejection of events. Any events, all eventualities. Analyst has absconded with her dreams – now the nights are punctuated by alarms, soggy sheets tossing her body into drugged sleep; or with all the lights on, scanning the supposedly familiar room, she stares in the effort of a recognition which fails.

Then scenes from a shattered book arise, the characters reproach her, stand mournfully around, refusing to speak since their words fall into a void – a place of disconnection. Except for Maggie. If she looks carefully, even for an instant, it is shadowy figures of the men she sees, crystallized in Maggie in limbo, the soft resin of muteness. So, far from Analyst's probe, but not from the unpleasant awareness of Maggie's incessant, unintelligible murmur struggling to penetrate, to thrust its way into a shape of language; her resistance is porous.

Grasping the outline of the analytic ordeal, the skeleton if not the flesh, she is impressed that this question of the men, the characters, the book, had remained essentially dormant in the presence of Analyst's non- committal, non–committed utterances.

In fact the purposeful avoidance revolved, circulated, toxic blood in the system of disclosure, of the narrative development. Alex is frozen, unregenerate, certainly lopsided, his face shifting without notice. His milder version is Paul, a false whitewash; another form of avoidance, a quick cover–up. Jean–Claude, evaporating, perpetually fading, erasing himself, being erased by the author, by Angelica and by Alex, is difficult to find, to locate as he wanders in India or Nepal, condemned to mourning, to loss, bereft.

Inertia stalks each movement, yet even without the key, the mechanism manages to arrive at a pastry shop although the odor of food is exotic. It is a mystery that the waitress hears her order, hears what she wants in the lacuna of desire. Yet the sight of the world, of people, fills her with a nameless nostalgia.

And Angelica states that it was a love story. A love story without lovers, she muses, without resonance, evading the shock of a recognition.

In spite of that, Angelica begins the letters to Alex, begins the book:

"I can see you with as puzzled a frown as you ever dare let your features fall into, flipping the pages to the end to see who has sent you this letter. Or maybe you knew all along that sooner or later, I would have to commit myself to words, casting them into your silence. As you can see from the stamps on this parcel, I am in Switzerland. I've been here six months teaching English and French to twelve rosy–cheeked, well fed little boys. I walk to school every day through fields, and apart from the rustle of hay, the only sound is the cow bells. The sea, the angry rocks of Greece, the white sun still seep through the green hills drowning peace. "

It is possible that if Angelica could have continued to write the letters, essentially love letters, the discovery of the tale could have unfolded. The letters however falter, stumble and disintegrate, adhering to an other story, she thinks now, an Other story of madness.

Significantly, although Angelica struggles, as Maggie says, though the glue of time and love, the letters cannot be delivered; are canceled by ignorance. Lack of address.

THIRTY

SHE IS OUT OF JOINT with the season. It is a wintry August, the ground unyielding, yet uncovered by the concealing snow. Winter fruits hide themselves, so she feels it now, under a baked cracked earth. Verdure, even water is a ghost, a chilled ghost wandering in the paths of late summer.

There is a terrible pressure, an unfamiliar urgency to accomplish an indescribable task before the Fall arrives, the fall backward, downward into tangled strands arranged neatly in Analyst's files.

This task seen through a lens, a long–view, compartmentalizes itself, refuses to join the narrative, become part of the story; won't fit, moves around the periphery. What, she wonders, does it carry in its wake? Possibly the pain, no not the pain, the grotesque shapeless words have no niche in language, are resisted, battle among themselves to annihilate their meanings, their very roots in the symbolic field of speech.

Flux of confusion supervenes often. The vantage point unaccountably shifts; from here to the Analyst's file, the careful notes, the tentative interpretations vacillating between arrival and departure, all seem make–believe. A fairy tale, an imaginary scene obscuring misshapen events, obfuscating the crippled words clamoring to enter.

Truly neither the Analyst nor the patient is anxious to have the play end; to see the audience lit up, remove the masks, the costumes in a small room of memories. It is confirmed by the incisive voice of Lacan: "There is a complete change of scene; it is as though some piece of make–believe had been stopped by the sudden irruption of reality."

Nevertheless another wishes it, interrupts, strangling the Analyst.

And in the unearthly aftermath, the ratty old woman can be seen, in her red and black garments traveling in a topography at once wood and desert; water and air, carving her path with her breath.

❋

the shape of her body has become a sign
fluorescent   in the black red as it swiftly travels
the breasts are cat eyes   the armpits pointed
ears   fur covers the stomach   the vagina is a
closed mouth sweetly showing small   white teeth
an unmarked grave awaits   the earth shuffled
by tiny animals   at a gesture of her   hand
the rest of the soft earth   forms two mounds
revealing the mutilated body of a young   boy his
eyes have been   sewn   together   his hands are
tied   in a knot   his lips are peeled back   on
toothless gums   his ears are   holes stuffed
with grass   he is smooth between the legs   and
his feet   are cut off

Ah now they are seen entering a cave together.
This is the moment the animals howl; the time for a

green lion under a black sun, with a red dragon under a black moon mating in the shadow of monstrous wings. Here the searching eyes are pierced, closing in a perfect sleep.

THIRTY-ONE

SEPTEMBER ARRIVES full of retrospection; the uninterruptible process resumes in a catalogue of reiterated events.

The fissures close, sealing the patient in the dialogue/monologue or triadic discourse by turns, rotating words, and often the patient is a thread spun by language.

This August absence, holding the fear of loss, instead proved itself a cornucopia, she is saying. A rupture which reversed the valences, and now, she grins at the ceiling, now the couch, the room, the odd noises, have fallen into a flatter space, a place of visible edges.

Is this all winding down, she wonders. Is the spinning thread returning to its source?

Not yet; the ceremony is not over. The spirits, the ghosts, the demons, still roam the paths, inhabit the house, speak out of the darkness of the earth. Then, this is a lull, a shapeless movement that precipitates fears, that heralds possible losses; the recollection of losses, the memory of what was an absence filled with other voices, other descriptions, other events cascading into lacks, sealing the cracks, closing up the abyss. So, the memory that veils the loss risks shattering in the face of silence, waiting for the rite to continue.

Well, this is the book isn't it? Maggie trembles on the verge of resurrection, unaware of the consequences of her death, she imagined that when the key turned in the lock, the room would enter her field, the walls would decay drifting away on the air.

Maggie, it seems, doesn't realize that she is a creation, a character, a denizen of Plato's Cave.

The Analyst is baffled by Maggie vaporizing; by her sudden substantiality as well. Still, Analyst is good enough, unconscious enough to participate in the continuation of the ritual. Analyst conceals her puzzlement, defends her interpretations to herself, consults the files as a reference; a stable signified.

Nevertheless, the patient spins her, weaves her into the book.

This book which stands on a precipice, poised for flight, but impatiently fades collapsing into pieces.

The men, she mutters on the couch, the men condemn the book, refuse it, mesmerized by Maggie they both reject characterization; are in adrenaline flight.

The heart, her heart in fact, palpitates in response. Is furious, struggles in the grip of the predator – is euphoric in the mouth of the lion. A green lion eating the sun.

A shield is being constructed in a cave.

A person in a room, lying on a couch speaks of a broken heart, an inconsolable loss, a death and resurrection past mystery.

THIRTY-TWO

AT LAST, BOTH THE ANALYST and the client cling to each other in a raft constructed of language, buoyed on speech, on words seeping, eddying around their feet. Vanquished or reformulated, the subject is reconstituted.

The madness of the subject, has it been understood?

The madness that hid in the psychotic episode of the Analyst's file, has it been returned, restored to the client? The actions shouting a past without time, speaking the truncated memory of absence, creating a negative which no solution can print, have they been grasped?

In any case, she twists around on the couch, staring at Analyst, who smiles briefly, concealing a question.

Yes, it works, this babbling in the dark. Maybe, she thinks. This isn't how it happened, she thinks. This turning to see a face, so familiar, a faint smell of perfume known so often and never recognized. Not at all.

There was an old woman in the hospital that first morning, mouthing her cereal. She seemed to say there was no exit, no passage, no pathway now that we had fallen here, dropped out of the sky, lost our wings. Without legs, consigned to crawl in these spaces.

Not so. Since at this point the raft splits, breaks apart, and the language is purloined from another text casting the Analyst into the client's sea. "You may think that you are engaged in looking for the patient's past in a dust bin, whereas on the contrary, it is as a function of the fact that the patient has a future that you can move in the regressive sense."

For the words of the actions, the speaking of the book, the syllables of this perfumed space, the language born as legs and arms, incarnate, become a womb, embody a subject turning on a couch.

Not only that, she thinks. Because the book exists, inexorably moving to its end as language along with the fading of this space of the couch, of the files, of the drawings, of dreams told.

Meanwhile, the work continues as if nothing has been said. A dream has been brought, an offering. A snippet of an image, an engraving. A high tor, a sky behind it emanating silver through a dark glass; a woman wearing a red dress blowing in an unfelt wind seen from below; beside her a young boy seated on a black horse.

Still life

THIRTY-THREE

SUPPOSEDLY, SHE says, the book and this process are linked, although it is seldom spoken of here, from the pedestal, the soft lectern, the raised platform of speech. Because they both are a narrative, better a story, more accurately a tale similar to a fairy tale.

Consequently, if that is so, then although never entering into this dialogue, but inhabiting a space within the pages already written, the fairy tail of the two little princesses undercuts spoken language.

It's possible to say that the next frame is rolling into view, capturing the early morning hours while the body luxuriates without pain.

Long, long ago, remember the two princesses?

Well, you recall that they agreed to separate from each other. The one determined to wander, to journey to the ends of the earth to find the young man so cruelly tormented by the evil magician who usurped the throne. She found numerous friends along the way, acquiring fabulous treasures full of magic. The cloak of invisibility was the most treasured since it protected her from the gaze of the evil King. But alas, when she arrived at the ends of the earth, she discovered from an ancient troll, hideously ugly, who recounted a queer tale, that the young man was gone.

The Tale of the Hideously Ugly Troll

Spoken from the ends of the earth into the Ear of the Princess

I haven't lived here all my life, you know. No, not at all. And I wasn't always so ugly either. Oh, I know I am Hideously Ugly so don't get embarrassed and pretend you didn't notice. But anyway, you want to know about that young man not about me. But they go together, you see the paths entwined, got all mixed up in fact after he arrived. Or maybe it was before.

My mother was beautiful, as beautiful and full as the moon, at least I think so. But sad to say, when I was born she became ill with a terrible sickness and the only way to cure her was to become Hideously Ugly. So I agreed, thinking that afterwards, I could change it all back. Afterwards when she was cured. However, it didn't work. No matter what I tried I stayed as you see me now. Then I found this place at the end of world to hide myself in. All I did was read and think about how to get it all straight again until one day the young man came here, almost in pieces, blown here by the evil King. He could hardly see or hear because the violent wind breath of the King had banged him to a pulp.

So I took care of him and hid him in a cave until

he was all better. We talked all the time and then it came to light that there existed a way to help us both. Being a Hideously Ugly Troll at the ends of the earth, I knew of a priceless gem created before the beginning of time, hidden in the bowels of the earth. I could never get it because although the trolls know of it, it is proof against us, you see, otherwise there would be no priceless gem, you see? But a human can grasp it, only they never know where it is.

Anyway, he isn't here because he's there, under the earth, in the hole I dug for him at just the right spot, getting the gem. There's no time there at all, and what is even queerer is that when he comes back, no time will have passed for him, but we might wait and wait here until we are old and gray.

After hearing this tale, the princess did not know what to do. She was unsure whether to stay or leave. She had a magic way of contacting her sister, which she did.

The ineffably sweet voice of her sister spoke to her out of a floating ball that appeared quite suddenly, startling the Hideously Ugly Troll.

Stay, sister, you have done well. Stay there at the end of the earth until the young man returns, then the dance will begin that will weave the evil King a coffin.

A coffin of lead that will burn forever at the bottom of the sea, guarded by those who raised us.

Hearing this, the princess was overjoyed vowing to wait, even as long as eternity, for the young man to return. To wait for a dance that will set the wheel spinning.

THIRTY-FOUR

NOW THAT REALITY, at first unknown, unimagined, then a nightmare, then an invasion, has finally rendered all other realities pale, flimsy, insubstantial; imagination is left with only whispers, unheard in the cacophony of these real events, subsumed, subverted, shut out and shut up, the realm of images defends its few scattered, treasured inventions ...resistant, deaf.

The ego grinds itself up daily, pastes itself together in the semblance of a persona, patches the holes hourly, shows its muscle, demonstrates its prowess in an increasingly smaller space, contracted and far from home, actually homeless, it wanders not on a pilgrimage, but in ever decreasing circles. Towards?

Isn't this supposed to strengthen, to shore up, to through words re–create, restore? Instead, some story suddenly speaks itself, interrupting this discourse, casting it adrift again, sabotaging this remodeling.

It all has to be factored in, that is the aim of the analysis, that is the intention of an other, engaged in a ceaseless battle, colors constantly changing, banners obscured in the wind, fallen on the ground, trampled by running feet. Too many alliances, too many false truces to make any sense; a field of black tents.

And this one here, she who stands at the crossroad, unready to choose, dispersed in realities, attempting to fashion a workable hallucination, cannot figure it out, is caught in an elemental equation.

The Analyst waits with her, making marks on a pad sometimes afterwards, sometimes while the client is crushed under the weight of words. The Analyst reconstructs a story for the file cabinet.

She, meanwhile, is ashamed to admit, to confess that she refused dismemberment. Yet, nevertheless she fell apart, became pieces of a conundrum.

She realizes, astonished, that there is a pathway to comprehend the extremities, to swallow the madness, to locate the still living events inscribed in acid on the slate of memory written by an other. But no road opens through to the jungle of hopeful imaginings grasping her, evading the light, still hiding.

He called again, she is saying, yesterday. He said he spoke to his mother–in–law, (she can be that if not my mother) causing him to agree with this analysis at last. He finds her baffling, infuriating in her innocent insistence, her perpetual disbelief, her territorial narcissism. Perhaps, he thinks, the slide show should be presented to her after all. It wouldn't matter, would it, if we did present it, she said into the phone. The mother will dance through it, in her tutu, eyes closed in an ecstasy of perfection.

Now that he sees her and by extension the truth of this analysis, he can begin to grapple with his own demons, by a queer osmosis they have heard the trumpets sounding through the wire of the telephone. He sounds, she is saying, as though his moorings have slipped into the sea. Both mothers stand on the shore inventing a family outing oblivious to his cries, they smile charmingly at each other; –a picnic perhaps complete with photos for the album. Luminous pictures, images as proof to hold up to the frailty of words. His mother is only worried about the money. Not her money to worry about. The mothers reveal themselves as outside this story.

Shall she go down to the sea, slipping on the rocks where she sees his hand held out at last or shall she, instead, go to the shore to sit in the blue beach chair under an umbrella, wearing a sun hat, moving in slow motion to face the camera as it snaps her image, creating a paper truth.

It is so tempting to believe it, she thinks, feeling her cheeks wet. Almost to believe it is the salty sea air. It is so convincing, this eternal moment of canned happiness; three women on the beach. Beached.

How can this speaking now efface those prints, imprinted in the black box?

The Analyst mutters on, interpreting the transference.

She, the client, digs in her heels. She knows that the book, the madness, the analysis, the searing events, the charred flesh can become ashes blown away on the wind of a dream of a photograph album.

So then, this is grief. It has no tale to tell in this room. Her heels slide, slipping on sea–sprayed bedrock. There is a smell of something burning.

THIRTY-FIVE

IT, THIS PROCESSIONAL through the inner dimensions, clearly and obviously without end, is telegraphing the end. She is not ready. Not prepared to terminate, or be terminated. Nevertheless she broaches the subject. Instantly, she finds herself sitting up on the couch, warily observing the Analyst. The cells rebel turning her blood to a frozen red wasteland, while her voice continues to utilize logic. The logic of escape, of pretense. She can hear it abundantly, if unwillingly, as the sound of the words, this tinny utterance resonates and is submerged in a panic believed to have been dismantled.

She is compelled to attend to the clarity expressed by the abandoned body. Not ready at all. She wishes, fervently desires to know the outcome; is terrified to grasp that the end is in sight, is coming, bounding towards her from the black hole of the future. Prefers instead to construct a reasonable story, a likely story; and is simultaneously alert to the dangling threads, the unfinished business of narrative(s) lurking moodily in the room.

For the instant she rises from the couch for the last time and says goodbye, everything she spoke, or dreamed, saw in the pit of her body, rescued from oblivion, all the words too heavy to lift, the multitude of silent watchers, all of it will have been so. Will have been forever the truth.

Analyst is thunderstruck by the notion of terminating. However she remains calm, slowly, carefully slackening the line. After all, the Analyst feels the hook in her mouth as well. She is cautious with reason.

The client gratefully lies down on the couch once more and resumes the discourse, the babbling. But it has been altered, subtly changed; there is a tugging, a tug of war in progress now, an activation of the pull, the push toward separation/release from the bondage of speaking. The fright at seeing her own face at last.

Without a mirror.

Without light.

To listen to the sound of her voice, alone, and to hear the other voices finally freed, finally in the uncanny quiet enunciating truth, being reality.

Even able to have a language of desire.

That night, for the first time, she has a dream outside the frame of the small shared space, the heated temenos. A dream she can (will she?) tell as her own.

She is with a friend at her house and they suddenly hear the pounding of enormous wings close to the roof. They run to a ladder which leads to a parapet, behind which they can hide. Above them, a gigantic prehistoric bird/mammal dragon lands gently on the roof. They are trembling with fear but continue to watch as this enormous beast lifts one of its taloned legs and slowly carefully makes a perfect vertical incision in its scaly breast. Then reaching in, it grasps the still beating heart and raises it to the massive mouth, consuming the heart, alive with an incandescent redness. She and her friend watch paralyzed, with their mouths' agape.

Awakening, the thought is of sacrifice. A sacrifice beyond human comprehension. An omen, this falling beast bringing a message still to be decoded, still to be woven into the finale, the imminent closure of the book, of all the narratives, the tales and above all the analysis.

THIRTY SIX

IT IS FOREVER THE beginning, the start again of a new landscape, where then to begin this ending?

There are a multitude of dreams, fragments of images documenting a re–construction, a remodeling. There is a street in New York, she is walking to a place, but the place is boarded up, hidden from view, huge signs announce the site as under construction. Anyway, she peers through a hole in the boards and sees frantic scurrying workmen hammering, painting a large building, a house. Another time she is standing on a scaffold putting together a gigantic map of the United States, each state a different color. It isn't finished yet; there are still spaces left vacant. Again, she wanders through a brand new house, with rooms still without a roof, in the back of which there is a steep rocky drop to the sea, not navigable as yet, but far below she can see two fishermen casting their nets and a number of workers beginning a precarious stair-walk up to the house.

Well, she is saying, there is activity, but nothing is happening here, up above, in the daylight world of the endless discourse. Nothing at all. An eerie calm, unsuspected and suspect. She has no concept of what to do in non–movement, what it may signify. Death, she thinks, it feels like death this quiet without comfort.

Long ago, the comfort came somehow from an unseen space, uncontrollable, her own wish masked by a despair so intense it left no trace. It arrived without warning, without objects, without faces, allowing her to drift away to still unremembered places. This comfort only left great gaping holes, ripping the weaving of her childhood into a few threads.

Now it is different, she thinks. Now there is someone there (is there someone there?) who is not at all obvious, who is nevertheless present though being paid. Consequently the threads left are being woven and the lacunas too, vibrating with unearthly colors, colors never named or seen. Becoming a part of the narrative without saying a word, there is no sound for that story, no song at all, except of a wonderment in the ears.

It is possible, she thinks, it is even likely, that when gazing into the mirror at her naked body, so there, so integral in the mirror, so without evidence she can see it and is filled with awe. Baffled.

Where before, at the point along the trajectory of an exploding psyche, a body in bits and pieces, along the pathway of the released storehouse of memory, she often, usually, used this mirror–image to pretend that it spoke the truth; that the surface belied the interiority of the truths it was spewing forth in a cataclysm of memory.

Now all that is abundantly clear; the fire of remembrance, the blazing inscriptions have burnt dry, have reduced to powder any hope of argument.

And Analyst. What of her? She knew, did she know, that this would be the resolution, that this was the intention of the talking–cure? This startling outcome of a reality etched in stone, (foreseen from the very beginning, from the first sight of the roundness, the smoothness of the stone she, the client, encountered at that first session) she now realizes, was her goal. To carve reality into the stone–flesh of this dialogue, to re–construct a base rooted in the earth of heaven. Her own root having been dissolved in the acid of torture.

Analyst dreams of theories, doubts memory, is tangled in a web, cannot grasp the language spoken here in a foreign country consulting an old guide book. It doesn't matter. She is the block, unwittingly, on which the narrative will have been written by an Other.

In the stream of consciousness, free falling, hang–gliding on the syllables issuing from her mouth, she suddenly hears her voice.

She is saying: How peculiar that being mad, if that's what it was after all, having a pathology, is somehow described in your DSM IV. But the guide book is meaningless, has suddenly no significance, has altogether vaporized. Has become another thread in this fabric, another tale in the book. And the story of the island, which appears again as it was, white in the Greek afternoon reflecting the sheen of the sea around it, continues the struggle that was abandoned when Maggie fell. The camera carefully focuses on the figures, still too far away to be seen, laboriously making their way to a white hot church glittering in the sun at the top of a rocky hill.

THIRTY-SEVEN

IN FACT SHE WAKES up one morning to recognize that in spite of the intensity of lying on the couch, she has been able to move outside in the daylight world, increasing the exercise of falteringly becoming a dimensional person.

That, in fact, on this wintry day waiting beyond the window, with its trees hopefully stoic, warm at the root, she is able to quietly regard the scatter of papers, now in neat piles arranged on the table. She has surprisingly not been idle.

It is obvious that the book has only ever been Notes, fragmented in catastrophes; that it will have to be just that, remain alive bearing the marks of its wounds, its lacks, homeless. Never to be a real narrative. Only to become part of something greater than itself. So without struggling to pretend a form; to shape a clay figure in a mirror, the anxiety subsides and she begins to read the last stack of papers, set aside because the middle fell out; erased before they might have been written.

"Angelica has not been idle, waiting in New York, heavy with the ghost of Maggie. Fearful of forgetting that Maggie was gone; horrified at the specter of the loneliness; yet burdened by the terrible presence of her no longer being there. So she writes:

"In the smoky confusion of grief I wanted Alex to have been implicated, to have somehow caused Maggie's death. It made it more understandable. I believed she would never abandon me, no matter how far away she went I somehow thought she would always be there, that her laugh would be a reality. Now it is only an echo, a sound I can hear as I fall asleep, it is no longer connected to the world."

Tangled in Angelica's grief, she sees now that the creation, the transformation of Alex into Paul, was a detour. An attempt to render him acceptable at least amenable to a dialogue, to capture and imprison him, to make him palatable. To whom, for whom this reconstruction of character, she ponders now staring at the words?

"The belief in Paul as real was one more ploy to postpone the advent of grief; to avoid the deconstruction of Alex the mythos of a seeming correspondence. To embalm the image Angelica first thought she saw at the harbor the moment that they met; to delay the dismantling of the instant Maggie disappeared. Since it would have been necessary to immediately grasp that Alex was lost to Angelica as well, sitting in Rome swinging his leg, perpetually on the loose, available and free. A caricature of Maggie.

"No matter what I did after Maggie disappeared, it was designed to recapture her. To find her shadow in Alex. To agree that he could reflect, when all along it was Maggie's face I sought. Insistently hoping for her re–appearance, her moon smile in the night. Maggie's collection of masks might have warned me, but by what peculiar reversal had Alex become Maggie's mask to ward off the inevitable.

"Then Alex was Maggie's magic act. She wrote him that day at the dock because she was lonely and full of terrible apprehension that soon she would be no more. She wrote him for me, her sister, because I was depressed.

"So that I might see, in Maggie's reflected light, my own face at last."

Now the time, the point has been reached, for Maggie's funeral to be written. From here in New York, Angelica discovers that Jean–Claude has returned. Honed by his travels, his exile, his outline becomes a possibility. And even Alex can be located, has left a trace, a small remnant of Maggie's glamour.

"So we see them from a great distance, on that day, in a circle, black on white, as Maggie is lowered into the earth. There is a spot, a flash of red as the flowers fall and the circle breaks. Alex with his scuffed shoes shakes the hand of Jean–Claude and starts off down the mountain, receding, diminishing in the glare of Greece. Jean–Claude stands in sharp silhouette; poised.

And Angelica, bathed in tears composes the end of this story:

"Maggie – I received your message this morning, this YES which I stare at trying to divine its manifold tendrils, its sweet aroma, this flower of YES reaching out and folding in on itself again, a center hidden in some pollen beginning. Is it my turn? This morning before the trek up the hill, it seems I heard the muffled roar of a jet cutting into the silence of sheep. It broke the morning with a wild expectation.'"

THIRTY-EIGHT

THAT BOOK THAT burst in on me in Greece; and all the characters that danced with me in the madness seem to have written themselves out, found a point of termination.

Heralding this last day, don't you think, on the couch. The talking, the spout of words, of a speech that could only have been born outside the discourse of the world; articulating events banished from collective illusion has fashioned a lance, a movement of light illuminating the subject on the couch rising from a bed of nails changed into roses.

While far away at the ends of the earth a Hideously Ugly Troll and a beautiful princess wait for the return of He Who Seeks the Priceless Gem.

And a woman in a red dress with a young boy on a black stallion return to the people waiting for them, keeping the fire burning, now in a glade, now by the sea, now in a desert. They do not recognize her at first, mesmerized by her youth, until she passes her hand over their eyes, until they see the ratty old woman once more, smoking her pipe, feeding the fire new wood sprinkled with sweet smelling herbs.

And a woman on a couch in a city looks at another woman sitting in a chair holding a pad which she now lays down on the floor beside her. And they say:

It is interminable isn't it?

But nevertheless this is termination.

The fabric is re–woven and the light of words, these words of light will have filled in the multitude of missing events, of absent and irretrievable joys, of elided terror. This lance of reality will whirl in the air, spinning in ever greater spirals, cutting through to a victory, a winning in sadness; a victory that can say yes to the death of illusion in freedom. A singing lance that will burn to ashes the gaze of the others creating the poisonous photographs, that will have consumed the pictures captured in their looks; that forever swallows their words.

The two women stand up, their hands touch for the first time and forever, they gaze at each other and all the words have been said, the tale has been told. She departs the sacred space and the last we see of her she is walking down a street in the first moment of Spring. In the distance is a man with a small little girl.

Miraculously I, I can see this small child running towards me, her legs spinning in glee, propelled by life, racing into life, catapulting into my arms. I say yes to the smell of her, to her life, to her flesh and bones sweet as grass.

While elsewhere a ratty old woman resting by the fire says this story, this tale has ended.